PRAISE FOR *THE MESSENGER*

'*The Messenger* is an extraordinary book. It requires the reader to judge whether its undeniable literary power establishes its authority to attempt to awaken us, through the voice of a fictional Jan Karski, to a terrible possibility—that the reason Karski's message did not shake the conscience of the world was because there is no such thing to be shaken, no such thing as a common humanity that would show itself in the sympathy of all the peoples of the earth for evil done to their fellows. "With the extermination of the Jews of Europe," the fictional Karski declares, "the very idea of humanity died." I believe that it has earned that authority.

'*The Messenger* has already provoked fierce controversy in Europe. It could not be otherwise. It is a controversy we need and *The Messenger* is worthy of it, which is a fine achievement in itself.'   RAIMOND GAITA

'Strong and intelligent, a huge act of empathy. A brilliant book.'   JOAN LONDON

'Deftly crossing the boundaries between fiction and non-fiction, *The Messenger* explores what it means to remain human in the midst of extreme brutality and indifference. This portrait of a man of exceptional courage and nobility, who bore witness to the darkest crimes of the twentieth century, is both profoundly disturbing and uplifting.'   ARNOLD ZABLE

'A literary exercise of the highest order, which breaks the boundaries between fiction and non-fiction...'   *Le Figaro Littéraire*

'A troubling novel about the memory of evil...a brilliant book.'   *Le Monde*

the Messenger

A NOVEL

YANNICK HAENEL

AFTERWORD BY MICHAEL BERENBAUM

COUNTERPOINT
BERKELEY

'Who bears witness for the witness?'
PAUL CELAN

Born in Rennes in 1967, Yannick Haenel is the author of several novels,
Les Petits Soldats, Introduction à la Mort française, and *Evoluer parmi les avalanches.*
His novel Cercle won the Prix Décembre, and the Prix Roger
Nimier in 2007. Jan Karski (*The Messenger*) won the Prix du Roman Fnac,
and the Prix Interallié in 2009. Yannick Haenel lives in Paris.

Ian Monk is a British writer and translator, based in Lille. Since 1998, he has been
a member of the French writing group Oulipo. His translations include novels by
Daniel Pennac, works by his fellow Oulipian Georges Perec and a rhymed translation
of Raymond Roussel's *New Impressions of Africa.*

Mark Baker is Director of the Australian Centre for Jewish Civilisation and Associate
Professor of Holocaust and Genocide Studies at Monash University. He is the author
of The Fiftieth Gate, a personal book about memory
of the Holocaust.

Michael Berenbaum is a professor, museum creator, writer, and filmmaker who
specializes in the study of the memorialization of the Holocaust. He was deputy
director of the president's commission on the Holocaust and director of the
United States Holocaust Memorial Museum's Holocaust Research Institute.
For fifteen years he taught with Jan Karski at Georgetown University.

First published in French as *Jan Karski* by Editions Gallimard, 2009.
First published in English by the Text Publishing Company, 2011.

Page design by W.H. Chong
Typeset by J&M Typesetters

ISBN: 978-1-58243-814-6

Printed in the United States of America

COUNTERPOINT
1919 Fifth Street
Berkeley, CA 94710

www.counterpointpress.com
Distributed by Publishers Group West

10 9 8 7 6 5 4 3 2 1

IF WE ARE THE MESSAGE...

An introduction by Mark Baker

Facing the mass graves of occupied Poland, Himmler boasted to his SS officers that their deeds would be 'a page of glory in our history which has never been written and is never to be written'. The witnesses to this unwritten history had been silenced in the death camps, their execution in forested enclosures concealed by a conspiracy of euphemistic memoranda. Yet from deep in the earth the bloated corpses resisted oblivion and formed cracks in the soil, threatening to write their own version of history with the blood of their wounds. So the order was given to dig up the earth for a second time, exhume the corpses and incinerate them. The unformed words in the burned pages were returned to the ground or scattered in the ash that blew across the face of the world.

There were others who tried to write the secret history of those years before it was given the title Holocaust. Emmanuel Ringelblum, an historian from Warsaw, preserved fragments of ghetto life by burying archival documents in steel milk containers.

Members of the Auschwitz *Sonderkommando* kept diaries of their daily work and hid them beneath the crematoria. There were some who scratched out their testimonies on the walls of a gas chamber or on the ceilings of a freight train. Those few who escaped appealed to the living, or the not-yet-dead. Elie Wiesel describes one of the men who jumped from a train and returned to his village in Transylvania, where he was dismissed as a madman, a messenger from an imaginary inferno. Another of these unheeded messengers was Kurt Gerstein, who had witnessed one of the unwritten pages through the peephole of history: a hole in the door of the Belzec gas chamber where the Jews in agony could be heard 'weeping as in a synagogue' until they froze together like 'basalt pillars'.

Jan Karski first became a messenger for the Polish Underground but nothing could have prepared him for what he would later describe as his journey across the mythical River Styx that runs between Earth and the Underworld. Like a reluctant biblical prophet, he was tapped on the shoulder by two Jewish members of the Polish Underground, one a Zionist, the other a member of the Bundist socialist movement. They entrusted him with a message to 'shake the conscience of the world' and stop the murder of Jews. Their message was delivered in words and then in a vision which would forever be tattooed on Karski's eyes after he was smuggled inside the Warsaw ghetto and a camp he confused with Belzec.

Written in three parts, Yannick Haenel's *The Messenger* unpacks the transformative moments of Karski's life. It opens with a question informed by Karski's tortured testimony given in the 1980s for Claude Lanzmann's film *Shoah*. Haenel recounts the visual sequences of the film, prefiguring a major theme of the book that explores the inability to sever language from sight and action. We see/hear/read of Karski in his New York apartment, as poised as a Polish aristocrat, before the camera/reader/mirror. He is invited to give his testimony. Karski sobs, resists returning to the past and flees the room. Haenel's book is a meditation on this moment that forces itself on Karski—the impossibility and the imperative of remembering, what Haenel will describe as a 'silence that speaks' through the cracks of memory.

The second section is a description of Karski's book, *Story of a Secret State*, written in 1944. We learn how Karski wrote this book in a fury, dictating it in Polish to a translator and then directly in English, as though speaking the prophet's message in tongue. The transmission of the message is hindered by many obstacles: there is the problem of language, which Primo Levi taught demands a new vocabulary to defamiliarise us with ordinary words that have taken on a new meaning after Auschwitz—words such as hunger, cold, man. But the main problem that will haunt Karski for the remainder of his life is that a messenger cannot deliver a message without a receiver. *A Secret State* sold hundreds of thousands of copies; Karski obtained private audiences with dignitaries as high as US President Roosevelt. Yet people received his message with a yawn of indifference, animated in some cases by malevolence toward Jews, or by the inability to interpret the gap between the message and its commanding imperative. 'I cannot believe it,' said US Supreme Court Judge Felix Frankfurter to Karski in 1943. 'Do you think I'm lying?' challenged Karski. 'No,' answered Frankfurter. 'I just said I cannot believe it.'

Haenel wants to show that by refusing to recognise the message we have woven ourselves into its text. The message that warns of a crime *against* humanity has become a crime *by* humanity. It implicates us all, thereby redefining human history. And this is the point of the third and final section of the book, in which Haenel himself becomes Karski by assuming his voice in the first person. It constitutes a leap of the imagination from non-fiction to fiction, an attempt to 'coincide brutally with the book in question'. Critics like Lanzmann will regard the invasion of those physical and mental crevices where Karski conceals himself from the gaze of the camera as the ultimate sacrilege. In Lanzmann's conception there is a point of unknowability, a divide that separates the eyewitness from the actuality of the past. That is the meaning behind Lanzmann's quip that, had he discovered archival footage of the death process, he would have burned it rather than permit the pretence that memory can escape its root-edness in the present. But Haenel is spurred by the ethics of the messenger—the belief that it is possible to eradicate the divide between time and place. The messenger must become the message by creeping along the cracks of silence and giving form to it through speech, vision, and deed. It is not too late, Haenel urges, to awaken humanity from its collective yawn and deliver Karski's message from the broken heart of the twentieth century.

Haenel offers several images for how we might dissolve the barriers between message and messenger, between their time and ours. He tells us that to overcome a fear of spiders one must become the spider. One can replay the life of Karski by becoming Karski. But is this the brazen conceit of an author? Is there any way, as Haenel writes, for the extermination itself to be reversed, which was the core of the plea embodied by the founding message? And here, Haenel resorts to religious mythology to offer the most radical notion of his book, indeed, its entire interpretative thrust. The message can still reach its audience, he suggests, because the past is not irredeemably dead. If we are the message then we can reverse the death of humanity by bringing ourselves back to life through our actions. The past, says Haenel, can be resurrected by 'rekindling a fire from its embers' and creating life through the word. In this sense, *The Messenger* offers a Christological account of the murder of Jews, who have (again) been nailed to the cross of history, enabling the promise of redemption from the fall of humanity. If Lanzmann chose to name his film *Shoah* in order to resist the association of the word Holocaust with its origins as a 'burnt offering', then *The Messenger* reinstates the Jews in their historical role as messengers, be it in the guise of Christ, or in a more Jewish attribution as the archetypes of Exile.

This is the ultimate message of *The Messenger*, shaped by an encounter between Karski's Catholicism and his Judaism. This is not a book one merely reads; it is a book one receives—visually, aurally, and existentially. This is a message delivered by each and every one of us, to ourselves. 'If a book does not change the course of history,' Karski/Haenel asks, 'is it really a book?'

Is this really a book?

Haenel, like Karski before him, desperately wants us to answer that question.

Mark Baker, 2010

NOTE

The words spoken by Jan Karski in Part One come from his interview with Claude Lanzmann in *Shoah*.

Part Two is a summary of Jan Karski's book, *Story of a Secret State* (Emery Reeves, New York, 1944), which was translated into French as *Histoire d'un Etat secret*, then republished in 2004 by Points de Mire in its 'Histoire' collection, as *Mon témoignage devant le monde*.

Part Three is fictional. It is based on certain aspects of Jan Karski's life, which I have gathered from, among other sources, *Karski, How One Man Tried to Stop the Holocaust* by E. Thomas Wood and Stanislaw M. Jankowski (John Wiley & Sons, New York, 1994). But the situations, words and thoughts that I attribute to Jan Karski are pure inventions.

PART ONE

It is in Claude Lanzmann's *Shoah*. Near the end of the film, a man attempts to talk but fails. He looks about sixty and is speaking in slightly awkward English. He is tall, thin and wears an elegant grey/blue suit. The first word that he pronounces is: 'Now.' He says: 'I go back thirty-five years,' then at once: 'No, I don't go back, no…I can't…' He sobs, hides his face, suddenly stands up and moves out of frame. The scene is empty, all that can be seen are shelves of books, a couch and plants. The man has vanished.

When he returns to his place, his name appears on the screen: 'JAN KARSKI (USA)'. Then, just as he sits down: 'Former courier of the Polish government in exile'. His eyes are very blue and brimming with tears, his mouth is moist. 'I'm ready,' he says. He starts talking in a formal tone of voice, as though giving a recitation: 'In the middle of 1942, I was thinking to continue my service as a courier between the Polish armed

Underground and the Polish government in exile, in London.'

This manner of starting his tale protects him from emotion: it is as if we are at the beginning of Dante, but also in a spy novel. He explains how the Jewish leaders, in Warsaw, were informed of his departure for London and a meeting was organised 'outside of the ghetto' as he puts it. We understand at once that this is what he is going to talk about: the Warsaw ghetto. He says that there were two people present: one a leader of the Bund, or Jewish Workers Party, the other a Zionist leader. He does not reveal their names, or where the meeting took place. His sentences are short, direct, encircled by silence. He says that he was not ready for this meeting, because at the time he was extremely isolated by his work in Poland. And that he was not well informed. Each of his words bears a trace of the difficulties he experienced at the beginning, when he moved out of frame. It is as if his words reflect the impossibility of speaking. Jan Karski cannot play the role of witness, which is being given to him, and yet it is his, whether he likes it or not. His speech broke down straight away because what he has to say can in fact only be said *in broken language.*

Once again, Jan Karski says: 'Now...' as though to say: 'How can I say this?' As though to convince himself that he is still very much alive, and out of harm's way. Then he corrects himself once more with his first sentence: 'I don't go back.' It is a sentence which he will repeat frequently during the interview: 'Even now I don't want...I am here...I don't go back in my memory...' It seems to be a way to protect himself against his own words, and against what they will reveal. He does not want

4

his words to expose him once more to the object of his tale. He does not want to relive it. That is why he emphasises distance so much: 'I wasn't part of it,' he says. 'I didn't belong.'

Jan Karski tells how these two men described what was 'happening to the Jews'. He repeats that he was not aware of it. They explained to him that Hitler was in the process of exterminating the entire Jewish people. And not just Polish Jews, but all the Jews in Europe. The Allies are fighting for humanity, they tell him, but they shouldn't forget that the Jews in Poland will be totally wiped out.

Jan Karski grimaces, his hands seem to be imploring, as if at that moment he is identifying himself with these two Jewish leaders, as if, as he speaks, he is taking their place. He describes how they paced around the room: 'They were breaking down.' He explains how: 'at various stages of the conversation, they lost control of themselves.' Just like him, Jan Karski, in front of Claude Lanzmann's camera. But, in 1942, he was just being spoken to; he remained motionless on a chair and asked no questions. He just listened.

Thirty-five years later, it is his turn to speak. He repeats what the two Jewish leaders told him. They understood his ignorance, he says, and after he had agreed to relay their messages, they started to tell him about their situation.

Claude Lanzmann then asks him if he knew that most of the Jews in Warsaw had already been killed. Jan Karski says that he did: 'I did know, but I didn't see anything.' He says that nobody had told him about it: 'I was never there,' he says. 'It is one thing to know statistics...there were hundreds of thousands of Poles also killed, of Russians, Serbs, Greeks. We knew about it. But it was a question of statistics!' Who knew? And how much did they know? 'We' knew—but who is this 'we'? Jan Karski 'knew'—without knowing. Presumably because we know nothing without first having seen it, and this is precisely what Jan Karski is about to say. Because the two messengers invited him to see for himself what was happening in the Warsaw ghetto, and offered to organise a visit for him. The Bund leader asked him to 'give oral reports' to the Allies. 'I am sure,' he said to Jan Karski, 'it will strengthen your report if you will be able to say: I saw it myself.'

On several occasions, the camera draws nearer to Jan Karski's face. His mouth is speaking, his voice can be heard, but it is his eyes that know. Is the witness the person who is talking? It is above all the person who has seen. Jan Karski's bulging eyes, in a close-up in *Shoah*, stare at us through time. They have seen and now they are looking at us.

Claude Lanzmann asks if the two men emphasised the utterly unique nature of what was happening to the Jews. Yes, Jan Karski says. According to them, the Jewish problem was unprecedented, and could not be compared to the Polish problem or the Russian problem, or any other problem. 'The Jewish problem is unprecedented in history,' that is what these two men told him. And so they had reached the conclusion that the Allies' response should also be unprecedented. 'Unless the Allies take some unprecedented steps, regardless of the outcome of the war, the Jews will be totally exterminated.' It is clear that the two men wanted Jan Karski to inform the Allies. For him to be their emissary. That he should bear witness in London to the fate of the Jews.

So, Jan Karski goes on, in that solemn formal tone which he perhaps feels is protecting him: 'Then they gave me messages.' In his Polish immigrant English, his international English, Jan Karski says precisely: '*Then they gave me messages.*' But this is translated in the French subtitles as 'So they delivered their message to me.' It is like a verse from the Old Testament: the angels have come to tell the chosen one what he has to hear, so that he can then make it be known in turn. On pronouncing this sentence, Jan Karski becomes a messenger. '*Then they gave me messages.*' The plural 's' can be clearly heard—there were to be different messages: 'To the Allied governments', 'then to the Polish government', 'then to the president of the Polish republic', 'then to the international Jewish leaders', 'and to individual political leaders, leading intellectuals...' Approach as many people as possible, they told Jan Karski, to the best of your ability.

Jan Karski now stops using only indirect speech, and starts relaying the two men's words directly, as if they are speaking through him. He no longer uses the past tense; he reveals their message—and transmits it to Claude Lanzmann. As he speaks, he grows animated, he raises his right hand, his eyes are lowered, sometimes he closes them, he concentrates. He has doubtlessly recited this message dozens of times, thirty-five years have passed, he has already borne witness, these are words that he has pronounced a thousand times, which have been turned over in his mind just as often, and yet here they are, being spoken by Jan Karski as though they are coming out of the mouths of the two men in mid-1942, announced in the present tense, directly, as if they, those two men, are speaking, and Jan Karski himself has faded away.

And it is at this precise moment that Jan Karski actually does disappear from the screen. As soon as he announces that he is going to relay their message, images of the Statue of Liberty appear. The words 'NEW YORK' come up on the screen. We hear Jan Karski's voice saying: 'The message was: Hitler cannot be allowed to continue extermination. Every day counts. The Allies cannot treat this war only from a purely military, strategic standpoint. They will win the war if they take such an attitude, but what good will it do to us? We will not survive this war!'

Perhaps the director of *Shoah* wants us to hear this message without our attention being distracted by the person transmitting it, for the message to be heard as it was originally announced, as if it is those two Jewish leaders in Warsaw who are entrusting it to us, because Jan Karski delivers his message to Claude Lanzmann, and so to the world, just as it was delivered to the world, that is, to the Allies, in 1942; he delivers it just as a messenger should, in other words by effacing himself, by conveying it in direct speech, in the present tense, as if it is coming out of the mouths of those two Jewish leaders in Warsaw.

And so, while Jan Karski is repeating the message that the two leaders asked him to transmit to the world on behalf of the ghetto, while he is repeating it thirty-five years later, tirelessly, his emotions seemingly intact, Claude Lanzmann decides to show on the screen a symbol of that world to which Jan Karski spoke back then, to which he is talking at that moment, and will continue to address, the very symbol of the free world, its emblem: the Statue of Liberty. Does Claude Lanzmann want to pay tribute to Jan Karski's *liberty* in this way? Or rather, by playing on the contrast between the voice and the image, to highlight the tragic difference between the battered Europe which Jan Karski is evoking and the striking symbol of 'Liberty enlightening the world'? Or between the suffering of Europe's Jews, as expressed in Jan Karski's voice, and what America actually did to save them? It is impossible to know, but as Jan Karski's sentences continue, the camera pulls away, in a back zoom that slowly reduces the statue, until 'Liberty enlightening the world' is no more than a derisory figurine lost in the middle of the waves, and, from afar, we can even wonder, as in Kafka's *America*, if what she is brandishing is a sword rather than a torch.

Jan Karski's voice goes on relaying its message: 'We contributed to Humanity...We are humans. It never happened before in history, what is happening to our people now...' To this message, meant for the world, he adds the pleas that the two Jewish leaders addressed to him, so that he would accept being its bearer: 'Perhaps it will shake the conscience of the world? We understand we have no country of our own, we have no government, we have no voice in the Allied councils. So we have to use services, little people like you are. Will you do it? Will you fulfil your mission?' Several times, Jan Karski repeats, in a broken voice: 'Do you understand it? Do you understand it?' without it being clear if he is repeating a question that the two men asked him at the time, or if he is asking Claude Lanzmann. Because, in the voice of Jan Karski repeating what was asked of him thirty-five years before, it is as if these words are being addressed to us as we watch *Shoah*: 'Will you do it?'

Jan Karski's words come from afar, they seem lost in time, condemned to hopeless repetition. Has the 'conscience of the world', as he puts it, really been 'shaken'? The two men who, in 1942, said to Jan Karski, 'Perhaps it will shake the conscience of the world,' had only that hope left, and they hung on to it. But is it possible to shake the 'conscience of the world'? And does what we call 'the world' still have a conscience? Has it ever had one? At this moment in the film, while listening to Jan Karski's voice, we know the answer is 'no'. Sixty years after the liberation of the death camps of central Europe, we know that it is impossible to shake the world's conscience, that nothing will ever shake it because the world's conscience does not exist, the world has no conscience, and that the very idea of 'the world' no longer exists.

'We want,' he says, 'an official declaration of the Allied nations that in addition to the military strategy, which aims at securing victory...the extermination of the Jews forms a separate chapter.' And, of course, while listening to Jan Karski's voice repeating the request of the Jewish leaders of the Warsaw ghetto, just as he recited it thirty-five years before in London and in America, we know that there was no official declaration about the extermination of the Jews.

'...and the Allied nations formally, publicly to announce that they will deal with this problem, that it becomes a part of their overall strategy in this war. Not only defeat of Germany, but also saving the remaining Jewish population.' Of course, we know that the Allied nations announced nothing, that they made no such thing a part of their strategy and that they did not save what was left of the Jewish people in 1942, or in 1943, or in 1944.

'Once they make such an official declaration, they have an air force, they drop bombs on Germany.' Why, the two Jewish leaders ask through Jan Karski's mouth, don't the Allies drop millions of leaflets to tell the Germans what their government is doing to the Jews? If, after that, the German nation does not make an attempt to change its government's policy, then it will be held responsible for the crimes that have been committed. If no such signs are forthcoming, then certain targets in Germany will be bombed and destroyed, as a reprisal for the crimes being committed against the Jews. May the Germans be told, they say, before and after these bombings, that they are taking place because the Jews are being exterminated in Poland. 'They can do it!' they say. 'They can do it!' Jan Karski's voice sounds so imploring that it is impossible to grasp if he is identifying himself with the pleas that were made to him that day, when he accepted to be the messenger of the Jews in the Warsaw ghetto, or if, today as he repeats their pleas, he is deploring the fact that they were ignored.

We still cannot see Jan Karski's face. Claude Lanzmann's camera films New York from the windows of an apartment. It is the same apartment from which he shot the Statue of Liberty: a back zoom, and we discover a desk, with papers, a telephone, some plants and a chair. Perhaps it is Jan Karski's office, because on the screen at the beginning of the interview, the words 'JAN KARSKI (USA)' appeared. Earlier on in the interview, he said: 'I have been a teacher for twenty-six years. I never mention the

Jewish problem to my students.' Jan Karski is Polish, he is speaking in English, he has taught in an American university, perhaps in New York, right there, near this office, which is perhaps his. Claude Lanzmann films the skyscrapers of New York through the windows of this office; we see the Twin Towers, then the Brooklyn Bridge. The American flag appears, the word 'WASHINGTON' flashes up on the screen. We see the White House, then travel around the Capitol, which is filmed from a car. Here, too, the contrast between the terrible words being pronounced by Karski and the images of the monumental composure of American democracy evokes a distance, a misunderstanding, a dialogue of the deaf. Who heard this message? Who really listened to it? Is it possible that nothing was done? Jan Karski says nothing.

Suddenly, the words 'THE RUHR' appear through the greyness and smoke of factories. It is no longer the parks and fountains of the American administration that we are seeing, but German steelworks, railways, roadways, a brutal world of blast-furnaces, chimneys, flames and the name 'THYSSEN' on a gangway, then on the facade of a factory. Jan Karski's voice announces the second message. The first one was for the Allied nations. The second is for the Polish government in exile in London. The message states that something is about to happen, that the Jews in the Warsaw ghetto are talking about it, especially the young ones. They want to fight. They are talking about a declaration of war against the Third Reich: 'A unique war in world history,' the message says. 'Never such a war took place. They want to die fighting. We cannot deny them this kind of death.'

While reciting the message, Jan Karski observes that he did not know at the time, in 1942, that a 'Jewish military organisation' had been set up; he confirms that the two men told him nothing about it. The message is addressed to the person they call the 'Commandant in Chief', in other words, the head of the Polish government in London, General Sikorski. The aim is to convince General Sikorski to arm the Jews: 'Something is going to happen,' the two men repeat via Jan Karski's voice. 'The Jews will fight. They need arms. We approached the commander of the Home Army, the underground movement in Poland. Those arms were denied the Jews. They can't be denied arms if such arms exist, and we know you have arms.'

The third message is aimed at Jewish leaders around the world: 'Tell them this: they are Jewish leaders. Their people are dying. There will be no Jews. So what for do we need leaders... Let them go to important offices, in London wherever they are. Let them demand for action. If they refuse, let them walk out, stay in the street, refuse food, refuse drink. Let them die in view of all humanity!' And then, they repeat: 'Perhaps it will shake the conscience of the world!'

At the very moment when Jan Karski begins to deliver the third message, the words 'AUSCHWITZ-BIRKENAU' appear on the screen. A tree with dead branches, greyish earth dotted with weeds, a pile of dirt against a low stone wall. The camera moves on: it is not dirt but spoons, a pile of spoons and forks. Then a heap of shoes. Then others of toothbrushes, dishes, bowls, and tangled wires or hair. Jan Karski has just said, on behalf of the two Jewish leaders: 'We two shall also die. We will not try to escape. We shall stay here.' He recites the third message, while images of piled-up objects in Auschwitz-Birkenau cross the screen. And, at the end, he yells out: 'Perhaps this will shake the conscience of the world!'

Then Jan Karski's face reappears on the screen. He looks just as distinguished, but his face is now lined with fatigue. His eyes are lowered. There is a long silence. Claude Lanzmann films this silence. He says nothing, either. Jan Karski starts speaking again: he tells Claude Lanzmann that, of the two Jewish leaders, he felt closer to the Socialist, the Bund leader: 'Probably because of his behaviour,' he says. 'He looked like a Polish nobleman, a gentleman, with straight, beautiful gestures, dignified.'

This is precisely the portrait of Jan Karski himself. Because, from the very start, what is immediately striking about this man is his refinement—a wounded distinction. Time has left its mark on Jan Karski's gestures, but without softening them. On the contrary, the trials he has been through are visible in the dignified nervousness of his hands. An immense strength gleams in his bright stare: something like a cold intelligence, the determination of a man accustomed to remaining silent and living a secret life. The radical nature of an 'agent of the Underground', tempered by something softer. Because, in him, defiance is there alongside the hunted beast. He is capable of shedding tears and even of breaking down, as he did at the beginning of the interview, but his is a noble sensitivity: he is no bleeding heart liberal.

He explains how it was the idea of the Bund leader, the man he felt an affinity with, to organise a 'visit to the ghetto' for him.

This man calls Jan Karski 'Mister Witold'. We can assume that he was known by this name at the time, in the Polish Underground: 'Mister Witold, I know the Western world. You are going to deal with the English. Now you will give them your oral reports. I am sure it will strengthen your report if you will be able to say: I saw it myself.' He asks if he will agree to go into the ghetto, and then undertakes to watch personally over his safety. Once more, Jan Karski falls silent.

The name 'WARSAW' then appears on the screen, along with images of the city. It looks dead—a ghost town. Was the ghetto there? There is nothing left. It is the middle of the city, downtown Warsaw, and yet the streets look flattened. The buildings appear empty, frozen, deserted.

Jan Karski's voice picks up the thread of his story again, while the camera slowly films wastelands, ruined facades and abandoned houses: 'A few days later, we established contact. By that time, the Warsaw ghetto as it existed in 1942 until July did not exist anymore.' The camera approaches a house, with a sign: '40, UL. NOWOLIPKI'. *Ul* is the abbreviation of *Ulica*, which means 'street' in Polish. We hear Jan Karski saying: 'There was a building…the wall which separated the ghetto from the outside world was a part of the back of the building. So the front was facing the Aryan area. There was a tunnel. We went through this tunnel without any kind of difficulty.' He tells how the leader of the Bund, the 'Polish nobleman' as he calls him, had metamorphosed. 'He is broken down, like a Jew from the ghetto, as if he had lived there all the time.' On the screen, we can see an alley between two buildings. The camera moves down it. The tunnel comes out in a narrow, dark courtyard, containing the entry to a cellar. Another opening leads out into a large wasteland, full of reddish weeds, bordered by old buildings, rows of houses and brick walls.

Then Jan Karski reappears on the screen, very calm, talking about his guide: 'So we walked the streets. He was on my left. We didn't talk very much...' From here on, we enter into the heart of Jan Karski's tale. Everything that has been said so far was just a preamble. The real message that he has to transmit is not the appeal for international assistance, which he was made to learn by heart, nor the demand by the Jews in the ghetto for arms; the real message has not been articulated, or prepared beforehand then learnt by rote; there will be no ready words, it will be up to him to find the right words to express what he has seen.

We remember Jan Karski's hesitations at the beginning of the interview, and his refusal to cross that line of memory, as if there were a frontier between his present life and that horrible past to which he is incapable of returning: 'No, I don't go back... no...' He got stuck right at the start of the interview; he did not want to go back, even in language, inside the ghetto. There were no more words, he remained on the threshold.

'I didn't know this,' he says to describe the ghetto, 'I was never in a ghetto. I never dealt with the Jewish matters...' And so, now Jan Karski has arrived at that point where, for him, language has become petrified, he warns Claude Lanzmann: 'Well, so what? So now comes the description of it, yes?' This question is not really directed at Claude Lanzmann. It just gives a little respite to Jan Karski, so that he can ready himself, and perhaps also to add a little effect. He says: 'Well…' The moment has come, and he must now accomplish his task. Quite visibly, he would rather not. He is once more on the point of collapsing, he raises his hand to conceal his face, he swallows his saliva, his throat tightens; it looks as though he is about to crack, but then abruptly he launches himself into his tale: 'Naked bodies on the street!' This sentence emerges like a spasm. No verb, a raw vision. Nor any description of the place. We have been thrown directly into the ghetto, struck by the bodies.

Claude Lanzmann interrupts him at once: 'Corpses?' Without even looking at him, Jan Karski answers: 'Corpses.' He continues with his tale, eyes staring into the void, almost popping out of their sockets, as if he is seeing again those images and does not want to lose them. He explains how he asked his guide why these naked bodies were there, on the street. The guide answered: 'They have a problem. If a Jew dies and the family wants a burial, they have to pay a tax on it. So they just throw them in the street.' Claude Lanzmann asks: 'Because they cannot pay the tax?' 'Yes,' Jan Karski replies. 'They cannot afford it.' He explains that it was the guide who was saying this, and how the merest rag mattered, so they kept all their clothing for the living. 'Women with their babies…' The sentence springs from Jan Karski's mouth, like a second spasm. 'Women with their babies, publicly feeding their babies, but they have no…no breasts…just flat.' Jan Karski describes what he came across, what he saw, all at once: 'Babies with crazed eyes, looking…' he says. Corpses, flat-breasted women and crazed babies, such was the ghetto that Jan Karski saw straightaway and which he is describing.

17

He is now using the present tense again, he has no distance from what he is describing. He did not want to go back but, without wanting to, he now has gone back, he is 'back there', in the ghetto. As he recalls the babies with crazed eyes, his hands rise to his forehead. He is on the verge of breaking down. Claude Lanzmann brings him back by asking him a question, a question which is phrased strangely and which Jan Karski does not understand: 'Did it look like a complete strange world?' 'What?' Claude Lanzmann rephrases his question, but it is impossible to make out if he says 'Another world?' or 'Was it a world?'. The French subtitles translate it as 'Another world'. Jan Karski corrects him: 'It was not a world.' He adds: 'There was not humanity.' A long silence. Jan Karski remains motionless. The 'crazed eyes' are now his own.

Suddenly, he resumes his description: 'Streets full. Full.' He explains how everyone in the street bartered their meagre resources, and were trying to sell whatever they had: 'Three onions,' he says. 'Two onions. Some cookies. Selling. Begging each other. Crying: I'm hungry.' Jan Karski's sentences are now breathless. They are short, one word, two words, no more. Earlier on, he articulated slowly the long speeches that the two men had dictated to him. Now, his language is lifeless, he is no longer trying to convince or explain, he will not be able to help anyone. Impoverished visions attach themselves to impoverished words: onions, cookies, eyes, breasts. Such words save no one. Jan Karski is picturing again his trip to the ghetto, but the children he saw— 'those horrible children,' he says, 'some children running by themselves, or with their mothers sitting,'—are all dead. Jan

Karski repeats: 'It wasn't humanity.' He tries to say what it was, he searches for the words: 'It was some...some hell.' This word, too, seems impoverished: 'hell', almost a conventional word, which seems to suit here, for the sake of something better, because Jan Karski can find nothing else and because, if he says nothing, if no words come to his assistance, he will remain stuck there, in this absence of words, and he will suffocate.

Jan Karski starts his tale once more and the sentences grow longer, they are back in the past tense: 'Now,' he says, 'in this part of the ghetto, the central ghetto, there were German officers. If the Gestapo released somebody, the Gestapo officers had to pass through the ghetto to get out of it.' Then, all of a sudden, the vision returns. Jan Karski grimaces, his mouth twists as he says: 'Now, the Germans in uniform, they were walking... Silence! Everybody frozen until they passed. No movement, no begging. Nothing. Germans...contempt!' And, there, to express the scorn of the Germans as they looked at the Jews in the ghetto, Jan Karski puts himself in their place for a couple of sentences. He says, as if he is one of them: 'This is apparent that they are subhuman! They are not human.' Then, suddenly, panic. Jan Karski tells how the Jews fled from the street where he stood. He and his guide rushed towards a house. The guide murmured: 'Open the door! Open the door!' They both went in, a woman had opened the door. They rushed over to the windows. The guide told the woman: 'All right, all right, don't be afraid, we are Jews.' He pushed Karski towards the window. 'Look at it! Look at it!' the guide said.

The vision flickers. It comes and goes in fits and starts. Jan

Karski describes the Germans in these terms: 'There were two boys. Nice-looking boys. Hitler Jugend. In uniform.' In Jan Karski's words, the two German boys are set in the past, the Jews in the present. 'They walked,' he says. 'Every step they made, Jews disappearing, running away. They were talking to each other.' Suddenly, Jan Karski says, one of them unthinkingly puts a hand in his pocket. Karski makes the gesture of drawing a gun. His face is very pale. He pretends to shoot, in an almost childish way. He says: 'Shoots! Some shouting. Some broken glass,' as if they were stage directions. At the same time, he imitates the noises, but the sounds he produces are clumsy imitations. His face has gone white. He trembles. He says that one young German congratulated the other one who had fired, and then they moved on.

'I was petrified,' Jan Karski says. And, as he pronounces these words, he becomes petrified once more. What Jan Karski feared at the beginning of the interview was precisely that he would be paralysed by terror, just as he had been on that day in autumn 1942, in the Warsaw ghetto, when he came into contact with death. He did not want to relive that, but he is now reliving it once again. At this precise moment, when listening to Jan Karski, we no longer have the feeling that a voice is emerging from his body; on the contrary, it is Jan Karski's body which is emerging from the voice, because it is his voice which seems to be revealing to him his own physical presence. At last he has become the person he was incapable of becoming at the beginning of the interview: not someone different, but a character within him who fits perfectly with the essence of speech, the witness. Is it suffering that makes a witness? No, it is speech, the use of speech. During this interview, as he spoke, something else has arisen inside Jan Karski's words: he has reached the nadir, the point where truth finds its own language and where language finds its own truth, where words are no longer just clothing but the body itself, becoming one with it.

So, Jan Karski then tells how the Jewish woman took him in her arms. He sobs as he says it. He says that she must have realised that he was not Jewish. 'Go, go,' she told him. 'It doesn't do you any good. Go, go.' He starts to speak again in that literary tone which he resorts to when he wants to distance himself from his visions: 'So we left the house. Then we left the ghetto.' It is the same way he talked earlier about his arrival in the ghetto: 'We went through without any kind of difficulty.' And so he concludes his stay in 'hell', as he puts it.

But the story is not over yet; the guide said to Jan Karski: 'You didn't see everything, you didn't see too much. Would you like to go again? I will come with you. I want you to see everything.' And Jan Karski accepted. He tells the tale of his second visit at once, he does not pause—he goes straight on. He went to the ghetto twice, but in his memory, the two visits form a single sequence, a kernel of emotion. With tears in his eyes, he continues: 'Next day, we went again. The same house. The same way.' This time, he says, he was less in shock, and more sensitive to other things, such as the smell. 'Stench,' he says. He repeats the word several times. He says that they were suffocating. Again, his sentences are brief, reduced to individual words: 'Nervousness. Tension. Bedlam.' A tear runs down his cheek. 'This was Platz Muranowski,' he specifies.

Jan Karski noticed children playing with rags. The guide told him: 'They are playing, you see? Life goes on.' Jan Karski said that they were not playing, just simulating play. Claude Lanzmann asks if there were any trees. 'A few trees, rachitic trees,' Jan Karski replies. He tells how he and his guide walked for about an hour, without talking to anyone. From time to time, the guide stopped him: 'Look at this Jew!' A man was standing motionless in the street. Jan Karski freezes so we get the idea. He takes on a dazed look, mouth agape, eyes staring. A 'petrified' man, as he put it earlier. Dead? No, the guide said that he was alive. 'Mister Witold, remember! He is dying. Look at him! Tell them over there! You saw it. Don't forget!'

They continued walking, for about an hour perhaps. Sometimes the guide pointed out a man or a woman, and asked him to remember them. He pressed the point: 'Remember this, remember this.' Several times, Jan Karski asked: 'What are they doing here?' And, each time, the guide replied that they were dying. Jan Karski describes nothing more, his story falls away, as though a void is expanding inside his words. He says that they kept walking, and that he could no longer cope. He has reached his limit: 'Get me out of it,' he asks. He no longer finishes his sentences. He stammers. 'I was sick...even now, I don't want...' Once again, he tries to shrink away from what he has seen: 'I understand your role. I am here. I don't go back in my memory.' Because what was happening to the men and women he glimpsed in the ghetto is as unbearable as it is incomprehensible.

'I was told that these were human beings—they didn't look

like human beings.' Jan Karski's testimony concludes with this terrible contradiction. The contrast between the living and the dead is not enough to give form to what he saw. There are no words to express it. This is why Jan Karski then repeats what he has already said to Claude Lanzmann: 'It was not a world. It was not a part of humanity.' What are human beings when they no longer look alive and yet are not dead? Jan Karski has now run out of words and yet he says that he made his report, he recounted what he had seen. In the end, Jan Karski uses only negative sentences to express himself: 'I was not part of it. I did not belong there. I never saw such things. I never...nobody wrote about this kind of reality. I never saw any theatre, I never saw any movie!' He and the guide left the ghetto, they embraced and wished each other good luck. Jan Karski's last words are: 'I never saw him again.' With the same brusqueness with which he had addressed his guide when asking to leave the ghetto, he stops speaking. His chest rises, he breathes deeply, as though after exerting himself. He looks exhausted, he stares into space. A nervous tic starts up in the corner of his mouth.

PART TWO

Jan Karski recounted his war experiences in *Story of a Secret State*, which was published in the USA in November 1944, and later translated into French as *Mon témoignage devant le monde*.

The book starts on August 23 1939. Jan Karski had just gone home from a reception at the Portuguese embassy in Warsaw. He was twenty-five. He had spent three years in what he calls the 'great libraries of Europe', in Germany, Switzerland and England. His father's death called him back to Warsaw, where he tried to complete his thesis. He felt carefree, spoke several languages, was a bit of an idler—the world was his oyster.

That night, there was a knock on his door. A policeman handed him a red card. It was his mobilisation order. Jan Karski had to leave Warsaw in the next four hours and join his regiment, which was stationed in Oswiecim, right on the German border. Oswiecim is the Polish name for Auschwitz. Jan Karski was sent to the barracks on this site where, nine months later, the concentration camp of Auschwitz-I was to be set up. As he had done his national service a few years before at the school of artillery officers, he became a second lieutenant in the mounted artillery (in other words, the cavalry). He did not take this mobilisation very seriously; he just saw it as an ironic occasion for a 'military parade'. But Jan Karski was also an 'enthusiastic horseback rider', so he enjoyed galloping off in his uniform, across the plains of Upper Silesia.

If Jan Karski was not really sensitive to the gravity of the situation, he nevertheless reported a rumour he'd heard, according to which France and Britain would stop Poland from mobilising, because Hitler was not to be provoked, even though the Nazis were openly getting ready to invade the country. For this reason, the red card was a 'secret mobilization order' and no public announcement would be made.

The train to Oswiecim was packed full of young men, like Jan Karski, who were off to join their units. And, at each stop, other carriages were hooked on so as to accommodate the newcomers. When he reached the barracks at Oswiecim, joining other reserve officers who had now been called up like him, Jan Karski shared their general optimism. The coming conflict seemed like a show: 'Germany was weak and Hitler was bluffing,' he writes. Poland was now going to teach a good lesson once and for all to that 'farcical little fanatic', as Karski's comrades called Hitler.

But, when the morning of September 1 dawned, and the artillery division was still asleep, the aircraft of the Luftwaffe, which had penetrated their lines without being spotted, bombed the entire region. Hundreds of panzers crossed the frontier and shelled to shreds the slightest obstacle in their path. In just three hours, the region was laid waste.

Jan Karski and his comrades felt lost: 'It was apparent that we were in no position to offer any serious resistance,' he writes. The order to retreat was given. The cannons, provisions and ammunition were all to be transported to Krakow. As they marched down the streets of Oswiecim towards the railway station, gunfire broke out: they were being shot at from behind some of the windows. Their attackers were *Volkdeutsch*—Polish citizens of German descent—who lived outside the Reich and who had immediately taken the Nazis' side, thus forming a sort of 'fifth column' throughout Poland. The order was given not to fire back, so as not to slow down the retreat.

At the station, as soon as the tracks that had been damaged during the bombing had been repaired, they at last set off eastwards, towards Krakow. The train was attacked by the German air force. Over half the carriages were hit. Most of the occupants were wounded, or killed. Jan Karski's carriage escaped untouched. It was the first sign of his luck, a good fortune that was to turn out to be stupendous—and which would allow him to cheat death.

The survivors abandoned what was left of the train and, in total disorder, panic and distress, continued their journey eastwards on foot. 'We were now no longer an army,' Jan Karski notes. Hundreds of thousands of refugees and lost soldiers ran into each other on the roads across Poland. They advanced slowly. The journey took them two weeks. Jan Karski and his comrades had not fired a single shot, but still wanted to fight. As they marched on, they hoped to encounter some 'line of resistance', which they could join up with. But there was no resistance, just a disaster: the Polish air force and its planes had been neutralised. The Germans had already occupied Poznan, Lodz, Kielce and Krakow. 'The smoking, abandoned ruins of towns, railroad junctions, villages and cities added to our bitter knowledge,' Jan Karski writes.

The troops had been marching for two weeks through ruins, when they learned that the Russians had also crossed the frontier. The information came from a civilian who had a radio. 'Had they declared war on us, too?' Jan Karski asks. It seemed that a message had been broadcast over the Polish frequencies— a message in Russian, Polish and Ukrainian—asking the Polish people not to consider the Russian soldiers as enemies, but instead as protectors. Jan Karski apparently had doubts about such protection. He wondered about the status of the Nazi–Soviet pact. Was it still valid? Any possible shifts in that agreement of course remained secret. But, for Jan Karski, one thing was now certain. Whatever changes may have occurred would certainly be unfavourable to Poland.

There then began an extraordinary scene, just two miles outside Tarnopol, a town in eastern Poland, situated in the southeast of the country, right at the bottom of the map, in the corner between Czechoslovakia and the USSR. Jan Karski carefully took note of the date: September 18. The scene took place on the road. The Poles were on foot. There was a commotion. A voice came through from a loudspeaker. No one understood what it was saying. A bend in the road meant that they could not see where it was coming from. They pressed on; some even started to run. Outside the village, further along the road, they could just make out a column of military trucks and tanks. One of Jan Karski's comrades managed to decipher, in the distance, a hammer and sickle on one of the vehicles. 'Russians! Russians!' he yelled out. The voice from the loudspeaker was now a little clearer. It was speaking in Polish. 'The voice we were hearing,' Jan Karski writes, 'was speaking Polish, Polish with not so much an accent as the singsong intonation we familiarly associate with a Russian speaking our language.' The voice, which belonged to the Soviet commander, was inviting the Poles to join them. Before long, the voice grew impatient: 'Are you or are you not with us? We are Slavs, like yourselves, not Germans.' The commander asked to speak with an officer. There was considerable confusion among the Poles, who were hostile to the Russians. A captain made up his mind to act. He headed towards the Soviet tanks, waving a white handkerchief above his head. A Red Army officer advanced to meet him. The two officers saluted each other, and seemed to be conversing in friendly terms. They walked towards the tank, from where the commander's voice still rang out, then disappeared from sight.

Jan Karski describes the Poles waiting, feeling 'utterly crushed'. The *Blitzkrieg* had completely disoriented them. They could no longer bear this wandering around. Some of them were on the verge of a nervous breakdown; others were lying down in a stupor.

A quarter of an hour later, a strong, assured voice could be heard from the loudspeaker. It belonged to the Polish officer. He solemnly announced to them that there was no longer a Polish high command or government, and that they should join up with the Soviet forces. 'Commandant Plaskov demands,' he went on, 'that we join his detachment immediately, after surrendering our arms.' Then he concluded his speech as follows: 'Death to Germany! Long live Poland and the Soviet Union!'

Total silence. Jan Karski and his comrades were stupefied. Someone started sobbing and cried out: 'Brothers, this is the fourth partition of Poland. May God have mercy on me!' Then a revolver shot rang out.

The man, a non-commissioned officer, had killed himself. The bullet went through his brain. No one knew his name.

Disorder now broke out in the Polish ranks. Everyone was gesticulating indignantly. The officers ran from one man to another, trying to convince them to stay calm and lay down their arms. The protests and disturbances were quickly stifled by the loudspeaker, which called everyone to order: 'Polish soldiers and officers! You are to pile your arms in front of the white hut surrounded by larch trees—on the left side of the road.' The tone of voice grew harsher: 'Any attempt to conceal weapons will be considered treason.'

The white hut shone in the sunlight. The Poles saw that, on each side of the house, there was a line of machineguns among the trees, pointing straight at them.

The more senior officers advanced along the road, throwing their revolvers in the doorway of the hut. The rest of the officers did likewise under the incredulous gaze of their men. When it was Jan Karski's turn, the sight of that pile of revolvers gripped him, like a symbol of the absurd. He grudgingly threw down his gun, regretting that he had not even had the chance to use it. The rest of the soldiers also laid down their weapons. The last man had barely done so before two Soviet units leapt down from the vehicles to take up positions on each side of the road, their sub-machineguns aimed at the Poles. The loudspeaker ordered them to line up. The tanks manoeuvred, swivelling their turrets, their cannons turned towards the column which, taking up a slow march, now lurched off towards Tarnopol. As Jan Karski writes: 'We were prisoners of the Red Army.'

The column passed through Tarnopol, under the sad gazes of its people, who had come out into the streets. Jan Karski felt ashamed. He considered escaping. Four ranks further on, one of his comrades made the most of a moment's inattention among the guards to slip away from the column and leap into the crowd, which absorbed him at once. Jan Karski looked out for a favourable moment to flee, too, but the guards were watching him. He still could not believe that this catastrophe was really happening: 'The rumble of the tanks,' he writes, 'the glinting of the guns in the moonlight, and the strain of peering into the shadows all contrived to make me feel like a participant in some eery game.' When he at last saw the train station, he finally realised that Poland had been crushed, that this 'eery game' was called war, and that he and his comrades were going to be deported.

Jan Karski had felt moved by the faces of the inhabitants of Tarnopol. He realised that the Polish Army had betrayed the people's expectations. With a sudden surge of guilt, keeping his eyes straight ahead, he threw into the crowd, as an offering, the purse in which he kept his money, papers and the gold watch his father had given him. He explains that he still had a little money, which was sewn into his clothes, as well as his most important papers and a little gold medallion of Our Lady of Ostrobrama, which is associated in Poland with patriotic insurrection.

The men filled up the station. They lay down on the benches and on the steps, or else went to sleep on the floor.

A long goods train arrived the next morning. The Russian guards pushed the soldiers into the wagons. In the middle of each of them stood a small cast-iron burner, and a few pounds of coal. A pound of dried fish and a pound and a half of bread were handed out to each prisoner. Before getting on board, they were told to fill up all their available water containers from the taps in the station.

The journey lasted four days and four nights. Each day, the train stopped for half an hour, during which they were all given their provisions of black bread and dried fish. The doors of the wagons opened, and they could stretch their legs. By the second day, they were in Russia. On the station platform, small groups of Russians observed these prisoners curiously. They sometimes gave them water or cigarettes. During one stop, a comrade of Jan Karski's who spoke Russian struck up a conversation with a woman, who gave him a flask of water. She then called the Poles 'fascist lords'. 'Here in Russia you will learn how to work,' she said. 'Here you will be strong enough to work but too weak to oppress the poor.'

They got out of the train and, in lines of eight, marched for several hours through the mud to a large clearing, where the walls of a former monastery had been turned into dormitories. Jan Karski did not realise it, but in fact they were in the Ukraine, and this camp—one of eight especially opened for Polish prisoners—was Kozielszyna.

Immediately, instructions were issued from a loudspeaker: the first thing was to separate the officers from the men, then, among the officers, sort out those who in their civilian existences were policemen, magistrates, lawyers or high-ranking civil servants. The loudspeaker called them 'those who had oppressed the Polish communists and laboring classes'. They were lodged separately, in wooden cabins, and it was they who were, like all the officers and the entire Polish elite, a few months later herded into the camp of Starobielsk to be secretly executed under the orders of Beria, the chief of police, then buried in collective graves at Katyn. The Soviets managed for some time to attribute the responsibility for this massacre to the Germans. With these 25,000 murders, the entirety of the Polish intelligentsia and any hope for the country's future were scrupulously wiped out.

Jan Karski and all the other officers were put to hard labour. They had just one obsession: escape. Getting outside the camp did not seem that difficult, but managing to find a train appeared quite impossible. Then the idea of having to cross a cold, hostile country whose language they did not speak discouraged even the most daring. They heard that an exchange of prisoners between Germany and Russia was in the offing: the Germans would send all the Ukrainians and White Russians to the USSR, while the Russians would release all of the Poles 'of German descent', as well as those who had been born on territories that were part of the Third Reich. But this exchange would concern only private soldiers. So Jan Karski could not hope to be included. But he did come from Lodz, as his birth certificate showed, and Lodz was part of the Reich's annexed territories. A soldier who could not benefit from this exchange agreed to swap uniforms with Jan Karski.

So Karski went to the headquarters of the camp and asked to be included in the list of volunteers going to Germany. He presented himself as 'Private Kozielewski, formerly a laborer, born in Lodz'. (Kozielewski was Karski's real name.) The next day, he got into a train and, along with two thousand other soldiers who had asked to be sent back, retraced the journey he had made six weeks before.

The exchange took place near Przemysl, a town situated on the new frontier between Russia and Germany, as determined by the Ribbentrop–Molotov Pact, which allowed the two powers to partition Poland. It was on a November morning, at dawn, in a field. An icy wind blew through the prisoners' rags. They had to wait for five hours. Most of them ended up sitting down in the mud. To protect themselves from the cold, they covered their bodies with reeds tied together with pieces of string. The Russian guards struck up conversations with the prisoners; they were amazed that they preferred the Germans to them; they put this down to ignorance or madness. They kept repeating: *'U nas vsjo haracho, germantsam huze budiat'* ('Everything is all right here—with us; with the Germans it will be worse'). Jan Karski had no illusions. He was pleased to leave the Soviet camp, but he feared the Germans. To his mind, he was escaping in order to join up with the Polish Army. He was convinced that some of its detachments were still fighting.

Some German officers arrived in cars. They inspected the prisoners and sneered. The march then continued for a few more miles towards a bridge over the San, a tributary of the Vistula. On the other side of the bridge, Russian prisoners appeared, guarded by Germans. As they passed each other on the bridge, a Ukrainian jeered at the Poles: 'Look at the fools; they don't know what they're letting themselves in for.'

So the Poles were now under the control of the Germans. They were assured that they would be well treated and would be given work. Another train. Once more with sixty people per wagon. More black bread and cans of water. The journey took forty-eight hours. Jan Karski's comrades thought the work conditions might be hard, but they were convinced that they would be freed. As Jan Karski writes: 'The belief that we were going to be freed had effectively stopped the slightest attempt at escape.'

They got out of the train at Radom, a town in the west of Poland. They were then shoved into rows and brutally marched off to a camp. There, swathes of barbed wire surrounded the place. The camp looked terrifying to Jan Karski. The Germans assured the Poles that they would soon be released. They also said that, in the meantime, anyone trying to escape would be shot on sight. Jan Karski realised that they were lying: they would never be released and it was now vital to escape.

The next few days came as a shock to Karski. 'For the first time,' he writes, 'I encountered brutality and inhumanity.' What he saw in the camp at Radom seemed to him to be 'completely out of the realm of anything I had previously experienced.' His conception of the world was shaken. There was no medical care, and almost nothing to eat. The guards were brutal, and the cruelty constant. Not a single day went by without people being kicked in the stomach or punched in the face. And not a single day went by without a man being shot to ribbons for allegedly trying to get over the barbed wire. Jan Karski discovered that death has nothing exceptional about it. And that it amounts to precious little. Above all, he discovered that the worst thing of all is not violence, but that violence is gratuitous. The sort of violence being practised here seemed to have no motivation, neither the desire to impose discipline nor even to humiliate. Jan Karski thought that it was part of what he calls a 'code'—an 'unheard-of, brutal code', as he puts it, to which the guards conformed without even being aware of it.

There, Jan Karski realised something mind-boggling: he understood that *evil has no reason.*

But, in the hell of this camp, a miracle happened: every day, over the barbed wire, someone threw parcels containing bread and fruit, and sometimes pieces of bacon, and even money. Everyone rushed to uncover these treasures in the undergrowth. Jan Karski was quick; he often managed to pick them up. But, more importantly, he succeeded in establishing contact with this mysterious benefactor. Using a broken pencil, he scribbled a note asking for civilian clothes so that he could escape. The next day, he ran to search the bushes and found a parcel of provisions containing a note: 'Cannot supply clothing because I would be seen. You are leaving the camp in a few days for forced labour. Try to escape when you are on your way.'

Sure enough, a few days later, the Poles were taken to the station without a word of explanation. It was impossible to escape on the way. They were crammed into cattle wagons, thirty-feet long by six-feet high, and the only source of light were four little openings placed at eye level. They were warned: 'Anyone who creates a disturbance or fouls the cars will be shot.' The carriage was then bolted with an iron bar. The train pulled away slowly.

Jan Karski had made three friends. They were with him in the same wagon. Like him, they wanted to escape at any price. They decided to wait until it was night. Their idea was to jump off the moving train through a window. Jan Karski remembered a trick he used to play as a child: three men would carry a fourth man at arm's length, then by building up a little momentum, they would push him through the opening, head first.

The problem was that they would need the help of some of the other soldiers, who would surely be punished because of the escape, and so would not agree to risk cooperating. Encouraged by his friends, Jan Karski got to his feet and improvised a solemn speech: 'Citizens of Poland, I have something to say to you. I am not a private but an officer. I and these three men are going to jump from this train. Not because we value our health or safety, but because we wish to rejoin the Polish Army. The Germans say they have wiped out our army but we know that they are lying. We know that our army is still fighting courageously. Will you do your duty as soldiers and escape with me to continue the fight for our country's sake?'

The soldiers were not convinced at all. Some of them looked at Jan Karski as though he were mad, while others sneered. Not only did they not want to escape, and believed that the Germans would treat them fairly and give them work and bread, but they were also absolutely opposed to Karski and his friends escaping, because this might put them in danger.

But Jan Karski persisted, he even threatened them: 'We do not intend,' he said, 'to spend our lives as German slaves. What will your families say, how will your friends act, when they learn that you have helped our enemies?'

Eight soldiers then decided to join them. A few others agreed to help them slip through the windows.

Night had now fallen, the train was going more slowly. This was their chance. One of Karski's friends stepped forward: one man took him by the shoulders, another by the knees and a third by the feet. They placed his head in the opening of the window, then pushed him out. Four soldiers managed to escape from the wagon in this way. Then gunshots were heard, and a beam of light swept across the train. Jan Karski was afraid that the convoy would be stopped. Four more men went through the window. More gunshots. One of the men had been hit, they could hear him groaning in pain. It was now Jan Karski's turn: he was pushed through the opening, he fell into the void, tripped, and his head hit the ground. He heard further volleys, got to his feet and ran to hide behind a tree. The shooting stopped. The train had disappeared.

Jan Karski tells how he waited for about half an hour. He was hoping to join up with his comrades, and regretted not having agreed on a meeting point with his three friends.

Someone was moving between the trees. It was one of the young soldiers who had been in the wagon. He was eighteen and trembling with fear.

Jan Karski reassured him: they had escaped from the Germans and would not now be pursued. Jan Karski wanted to go back to Warsaw, the young man too. They needed to find civilian clothes, a shelter and something to eat. They were in a forest, it was night-time, and it was raining. After inching their way forwards for three hours, they saw a village. Light filtered beneath the door of a house.

Jan Karski decided to risk knocking. An old peasant opened. Jan Karski asked him if he was Polish. The old man replied that he was indeed Polish. Karski asked him if he loved his country. Yes, the old man said, I love it. Did he believe in God? He did. Jan Karski then revealed that he and the young man were Polish soldiers and that they had just escaped from the Germans. With the same rather cracked solemnity that he had adopted in the train when addressing the soldiers, Jan Karski declared that the two of them were going to rejoin the army in order to 'save Poland': 'We are not defeated yet,' he said. 'You must help us and give us civilian clothes. If you refuse and try to turn us over to the Germans, God will punish you.'

The old peasant seemed amused by Karski's speech. He said that he would not betray them.

His wife gave them some warm milk, with two slices of black bread. Then they were shown to a large bed with blankets. It was the first mattress they had had for months. They slept until noon. When they woke up, the old man gave them two pairs of pants and two tattered jackets, while his wife served them another cup of milk with two pieces of bread. Karski and the young man left their uniforms in exchange, and offered a few zlotys, which were refused. As they left, the peasant told them that there was no more Polish Army. There were still soldiers, lots of soldiers, but no more army. This was not a German lie. They had heard it on the radio, and read it in the papers. Warsaw had held out for a few weeks, but had then had to surrender. Everyone knew that Poland no longer existed, and that the Germans had taken one half of the country, while the Russians had taken the other.

Jan Karski asked if there was any news about the Allies: were France and Britain on their way to help them? The peasant answered that he knew nothing about the Allies, all he knew was that no one had helped Poland.

The young man started shaking. He wept in despair. Jan Karski went with him on the road to Kielce, where he left him in the hands of the Red Cross, before continuing on his own to Warsaw.

❧

During the six days he spent walking to Warsaw, Jan Karski thought over all the events that had followed that August night when, like thousands of others, he had been given a little red card. It was now November, and a little over two months had gone by since his mobilisation. He realised that, during these two months, he had experienced one shock after another: bombings, captivity, exchanges, imprisonment and escape. He had not been ready for all that, but there was probably no real preparation for such things. This explained why he had protected himself by coming out with that insane speech about the Polish Army which, in his dreams, was still fighting, even though everyone knew deep down that it was all over. Because what had happened was not just a lost war, but the destruction of Poland. In Polish history, every time their soldiers had been defeated on the battlefield, their country had been annihilated: its territory divided up and its culture destroyed. And yet Jan Karski continued to believe that some resistance, however tiny, however secret, was still being kept up in Warsaw.

Everywhere, all he encountered were 'vast areas of devastation left by the *Blitzkrieg*'. The roads were crowded by long columns of refugees, who were fleeing their ruined towns. They had piled up their belongings on carts, and were advancing with the implacable slow gait of the hypnotised. When he could walk no more, Jan Karski managed to get a seat in one of those horse-drawn wagons. He knew how to repair harnesses, so he could be of real use.

When he reached Warsaw, he discovered that the city was in the hands of the Nazis. The metropolis with its theatres and cafés no longer existed. Instead, there were now darkened streets and graves everywhere. At the heart of the town, an immense common grave had been dug for unknown soldiers. It was covered with flowers and surrounded by candles. A grieving crowd were kneeling there, praying. Jan Karski learned that the wake was kept up from dawn until curfew, with people taking their turns, and it had been maintained ever since the first day. It was no longer just a homage to the dead, but an act of political resistance.

Jan Karski stood for a while beside the grave, then headed for his sister's apartment. He found a woman broken by sorrow. She had just lost her husband, who had been tortured by the Nazis then shot. This place was too dangerous, and he could not stay there long. He rested for a night, then the next morning his sister gave him some clothes, money and jewellery.

Jan Karski started wandering around the city, which he barely recognised, so much had it suffered from the bombings. He recalled that one of his friends, whose frail health had meant that he had not been mobilised, lived nearby. His name was Dziepaltowski. Before the war, he had been a solo violinist, extremely poor, entirely devoted to his art, with an integrity that Jan Karski greatly admired.

Dziepaltowski was pleased to see Jan Karski again, alive and free. He seemed extremely serene and full of energy. While Poland was going through a catastrophe, Dziepaltowski talked confidently about the future: 'Not every Pole,' he said, 'has resigned himself to fate.' Jan Karski could not see a violin in his friend's apartment. His friend told him that there were now more important things to do. Then he asked about Karski's situation. Did he have papers? Or any money? Jan Karski told him about his dealings with the Russians and the Germans. Dziepaltowski was adamant: 'What you need are new papers. Would you have the nerve to live under a false name?' He got up and scribbled a few words on a piece of paper on his desk. Jan Karski was disturbed by the highly energetic behaviour of his friend, whom he had always considered to be a rather absent-minded idealist, but who was now telling him to read, memorise then destroy his instructions. 'You are going to have a new name. Call yourself Kucharski.'

Dziepaltowski also gave him an address. It was the apartment of a woman whose husband was a prisoner of war. He could hide there. She was a woman who could be trusted, but he asked Karski to be cautious with her, to be cautious with everyone.

Jan Karski's curiosity had now been awakened, but his friend cut short his questions. He advised him to sell one of the rings his sister had given him and to buy a few provisions, such as bread, bacon and brandy. Then get some rest, go out as little as possible and wait. His new papers would be brought to him before long.

Jan Karski did not yet realise it, but his initiation had begun: he had just joined the Polish Underground.

❧

At the address Dziepaltowski had given him, he found a thirty-five-year-old woman, Mrs Nowak, and her twelve-year-old son Zygmus. Both of them were very quiet. The apartment was huge. The room Jan Karski occupied was pleasant, with a reproduction of a Raphael Madonna on the wall.

Two days later, a young man brought him an envelope. It contained his new papers. His name was now Vitold Kucharski. He had been born in 1915 in Luki and had not served in the army because of his frail health. He was a teacher in a primary school.

There was also a message from Dziepaltowski giving him the address he had to go to to have his identity photo taken. He finished by warning him that they would not be able to see each other for another two or three weeks.

Jan Karski stayed in the apartment, lying on his bed, reading and smoking. Looking for work was too complicated and dangerous. With his sister's rings and watch, he could survive for a few months. He felt devastated by the Nazi order that governed the city, and every day the life of its inhabitants worsened. And yet, he remained convinced that the war would soon be over and that Britain and France would soon liberate Poland.

Two weeks later, Dziepaltowski came to see him, informing him that he was now a member of the Underground, in which he himself played an important part. Jan Karski was to learn later that his friend carried out death sentences on Gestapo agents. And that, in June 1940, he would receive the order to assassinate a certain Gestapo member called Schneider; he shot him in a public bathroom, before being arrested, tortured and executed.

Jan Karski describes the man-hunts organised by the Nazis in the streets of Warsaw. The round-ups. Especially those in June 1940, when they ringed an entire block, arresting the passengers of trams, customers in shops and diners in restaurants, before herding them onto covered trucks. He claims that twenty thousand people were taken away like this. Most of them were sent to Auschwitz, which had just been opened about sixty miles away from the capital.

He describes the terror that the Nazis spread in the city, through the collective reprisals they inflicted every time any form of action was attempted against them. This issue is analysed in depth in his book and, by analysing the part played by the Underground, Jan Karski exposes the very real scruples he had. In December 1939, for example, a German officer who was in possession of some information about the Underground was shot dead at the entrance of a café in the town. The Germans immediately arrested a good hundred innocents who happened to live nearby, and executed them. It was in this way, as Jan Karski explained, that the Germans hoped to force the Underground to abandon the armed struggle. But it was not possible to give in to such base blackmail and allow the Germans with total impunity to enslave Poland. 'To abandon our activities because of these cruel tactics,' Jan Karski wrote, 'would have meant, of course, allowing the Germans to attain completely their objectives.'

~

For his first mission, Jan Karski was charged with going to Poznan to meet with a member of the Underground there. Before the war, this person had occupied an important position, and the idea now was to determine how the Underground could win over those people who had been under his responsibility. Poznan was in the territory that had been incorporated into the Reich. To go there, Jan Karski travelled under a German name. The daughter of the man he was to meet played the part of his fiancée. She had also assumed a German name and asked the Gestapo for permission for her 'fiancé' to come and visit her.

Poznan is one of the oldest cities in Poland, and is considered historically as the cradle of the country's independence. So, Jan Karski was devastated to discover a town entirely colonised by Germans, with German shop signs, street names and newspapers in the kiosks, where the Polish language could no longer be heard, and where Nazi banners and portraits of Hitler could be seen everywhere.

His 'fiancée', Helena Siebert, was a charming, pretty brunette, whose courage was said to be exemplary. She explained to him how the situation in Poznan, as in all areas that had been incorporated into the Reich, was completely different from the one in Warsaw and the rest of the central regions. This was because the only Poles who had been allowed to remain in Poznan were those who declared themselves to be German. The others had been chased away, or were living on as an underclass. They were forbidden to drive cars or take the tram. If they ran into a German, they had to step off the footpath to let him pass. For this reason, the Underground could not be run as it was in Warsaw. She explained how, despite her loathing for the Nazis, she had voluntarily adopted German nationality, so as to serve the Underground from the inside. Because there were practically no Polish patriots there. They had all refused to be registered as Germans and had left the region. Soon all the Poles would be replaced by German colonists; the Nazis were emptying out houses in preparation for their arrival.

Helena's father, who had refused to change his nationality, was living in hiding in the countryside. He and Jan Karski examined the question of the Underground; it seemed to them both that it would be impossible to recruit members there, unless they came from the central province, the *Generalgouvernement*. Jan Karski returned to Warsaw and passed on his report.

≈

His second mission turned out to be far more difficult. He was sent to Lwow, which was under Soviet control, to carry out a certain number of orders, before attempting to go to France to make contact with the Polish government, which was then in Paris, under the direction of General Sikorski. Thanks to the messengers who travelled in secret between Poland and France, a connection was to be established between the Polish Underground and the government in exile.

Jan Karski was now to become one of those emissaries.

In Poland, there was no collaborationist government, as there was, for example, in France. And, also unlike France, where the Resistance took some time to organise itself, and even longer before acting, Poland started resisting immediately.

All the political parties that had joined together against the German threat were represented. But the agreement they had made in September 1939, in Warsaw, was to defend the capital, and this did not necessarily extend to other towns. This is why Jan Karski was sent to establish a similar multi-party agreement in Lwow, before going to France to inform the government in exile.

It was in this context that he met with Borzecki, one of the leaders of the Underground, who was about sixty years old, sombre, methodical, and somebody who had held high-level posts in several Polish governments—one of those men who, in the shadows, shape the political history of a country.

His house was icy. Borzecki was wearing a coat and offered Jan Karski tea and biscuits before showing him to an armchair. Meanwhile Borzecki remained standing, pacing about the room, his hands crossed behind his back. He was a man who thought that 'God has placed us in a fearful spot. We are on the most troubled of continents between powerful and rapacious neighbors.' According to him, the fate of Poland was to be constantly plundered, to regain its freedom in order to lose it again.

Borzecki was extremely determined. He explained to Jan Karski that if things turned out badly, he would not hesitate to commit suicide. He showed him his signet ring: when he pressed a little spring, the ring's gemstone rose up to reveal some white powder. Jan Karski laughed and remarked that the Medicis and the Borgias had used this kind of expedient, but that he did not expect to see the same thing in Warsaw, in the twentieth century. Borzecki replied that times change, but men do not: there will always be the hunters and the hunted.

&

The long conversation between Borzecki and Jan Karski was about the organisation of the Underground and its political significance. For Jan Karski, it marked the beginning of his life *as a messenger.*

Borzecki had given Jan Karski a message for Lwow, then another for the government in France. He was to repeat these messages as accurately as possible. In a sense, it was an act of proclamation for the Underground: he was aiming to unite the parties around a common action, and to convince the Polish government in exile to support this action.

The first point concerned a categorical refusal to accept any form of occupation. The presence of a German regime in Poland had to be opposed.

The second point concerned the notion of a 'Secret State'—or an 'Underground State'—which Jan Karski was to use often subsequently, and which was to be not just the title of his book, but also its subject. 'The Polish state continues its existence unchanged, except in form,' Borzecki said. In his eyes, the Underground was far more than just an organised reaction against oppression, it was the continuation of the State. Hence the legitimacy of its authority, which the government in exile absolutely had to recognise.

At one point in the conversation, Borzecki affirmed that the Underground should have an army. He thus established the basis of what was to be the *Armia Krajowa* (or 'Home Army'), whose unceasing activities culminated with the Warsaw Uprising of August to December 1944.

Borzecki assured him that the political parties in the German-occupied zone had agreed to this plan; Jan Karski should now see to it that those in the Soviet-occupied zone did likewise. Jan Karski was to be informed only of the main lines of the plan; someone else would communicate the details. It is not good to know too much, Borzecki said—it is even extremely dangerous. He added that some people, including him, were suffering from bearing such a burden.

A conspiratorial atmosphere took over as Borzecki explained Jan Karski's itinerary. He would have in his possession a certificate from a factory in Warsaw stating that he was travelling to work in one of its subsidiaries, on the frontier between the German- and Soviet-occupied zones. Once there, he would enter into contact with a man who secretly took people into the Soviet zone. He was a member of a Jewish organisation. Most of the time, he helped Jewish refugees across the border. The Nazis had already started to take measures against them in the *General-gouvernement*, and more and more of them were now fleeing. Jan Karski would thus cross the border with them, then go to the nearest station to take the train to Lwow. Once there, he would make himself known at a certain address, thanks to a password.

As they parted, Borzecki warned Jan Karski that if he was arrested by the Germans, the Underground would not be able to help him. On the other hand, if he was arrested by the Soviets, things might be easier.

Jan Karski writes how Borzecki was arrested by the Gestapo a few weeks later, without having time to swallow his poison. They broke every bone in his body, one after the other, but Borzecki refused to talk. He was then shot.

๛

While awaiting his departure, Jan Karski tried to get used to his new identity: 'I carefully memorised the statement from the factory and held myself in readiness to be able to respond to questioning.'

His mission started very well. No inspections. Once off the train, he had himself driven in a cart to the little village on the German–Soviet border. There, he knocked on his guide's door.

He was then taken to the meeting place. It was in a clearing, with a small stream and a windmill. The group he was to cross the border with would not be there for another three days. Jan Karski memorised the location, because he was going to have to return there alone, and be on time: the departure would be at the stroke of six o'clock. Meanwhile, he took a room in the village inn. For three days, he tried to remain unnoticed by pretending to be ill and staying in his room. On the appointed day, he arrived early at the clearing. The others were already there. There were families, couples, old people, children. There were also two women carrying babies in their arms. They had a huge amount of baggage: bundles, bags and trunks. Some even had blankets and pillows.

The guide announced that they had about thirteen miles to walk, through the forest and fields. It was already night, but the full moon lit up their faces. The guide led the way, quite quickly, without looking either right or left; the others followed, wading through the mud, stumbling, grazing their hands and knees, and scratching their faces. They fell over, the babies cried, everyone dreaded a possible patrol.

At last, they emerged from the forest. The guide was relieved. He told them that they had succeeded, that they were now on the other side, and had crossed the border. Exhausted, Jan Karski and his companions threw themselves down on the damp earth.

In the nearby village, Karski found a hotel, then had himself driven to the train station. The journey went by without incident. No controls. He fell asleep and arrived at Lwow feeling rested.

He immediately went to see a professor whose student he had once been, and who was now the civilian leader of the Underground movement in Lwow. Despite the password, the man was wary. He clearly wanted more information about Karski. He refused to speak to him, and instead fixed a second meeting, two hours later, in the gardens of the university.

At this meeting, the professor seemed more relaxed. He sat down next to Jan Karski on a bench. Karski explained to him the plan of the Polish authorities in Warsaw. The professor approved of it, and had even pre-empted some of the details. He was ready to cooperate. In turn, he described the current situation there: in the Soviet zone, the conditions were very different from those in Warsaw. The GPU—the Soviet secret police—was far more efficient than the Gestapo. Less brutal, but more scientific. The activities of the Underground were thus severely limited. And any contact between the different undercover organisations was impossible.

The next day, Jan Karski saw the other leader of the Underground, who was in charge of the military wing. Despite the password, he refused to talk to Jan Karski. When he introduced himself and said that he had a message from Warsaw, the leader replied that he had never heard of him, and knew no one in Warsaw.

That evening, he told the professor about what had happened. He was not surprised. In Lwow, the GPU was so active that everyone was extremely wary. So the professor promised to spread the message and instructions as widely as possible.

Jan Karski informed him that he had been instructed to pursue his mission in France, by travelling there via Romania.

The professor advised him against this course of action: right then, the Romanian border was one of the best guarded places in Europe; a line of dogs made any crossing impossible. He would do better to go back to Warsaw and find a different route.

ॐ

At the end of January 1940, Jan Karski returned to Warsaw, before taking the train to Zakopane, his new point of departure for France. Zakopane was a village in the south of Poland, on the border with Czechoslovakia. It lay in the Tatras, the highest mountains of the Carpathians.

Here begins one of the most astonishing sequences in the book.

The person who would act as the guide for Jan Karski and the two officers who accompanied him was a former ski instructor. The trip to Hungary would be made on skis. For four days, the skiers, clothed in large pullovers and thick socks, made their way through the Slovakian mountains. Jan Karski experienced a sort of ecstasy. 'The snow,' he writes, 'was purple in the half-light, becoming pink and then dazzling white as the winter sun rose behind us.'

Each of them carried their provisions in a knapsack, because the group had decided not to stop in any inhabited locations. They had with them chocolate, sausages, bread and liquor. The snowy landscape thrilled Jan Karski; the headiness of the speed, the pure air and the reflection of the sun against the mountainsides gave him a sensation of freedom which he had forgotten since the outbreak of war.

At night, they would find a cave, or a shepherd's shelter. Then, when dawn broke, they would continue their descent. The fierce joy he describes cannot be found anywhere else in his book.

On the Hungarian border, the group split up. Jan Karski went to the town of Kosice, where a Polish government agent gave him some clothes and drove him to Budapest. During the journey, Karski noticed that his throat was sore, and that his hands and feet were bleeding. He had to take off his shoes, and it was in this state that he presented himself to the 'director', as he calls the main intermediary between the Polish government in France and the Underground in Warsaw. The director provided him with bandages and promised to get him admitted into hospital the next day.

Jan Karski stayed in Budapest for a week. He nursed his injuries, visited the city a little and, when his passport to France was ready, took the Simplon Express, which crossed Yugoslavia and deposited him in Milan after a journey of sixteen hours.

A second train took him to Modane on the border between France and Italy. Many German spies entered France this way, passing themselves off as Polish refugees or members of the Underground. For this reason, when a liaison officer interrogated Jan Karski, it was a real grilling. But once it had been established that he was on a mission for the Polish Underground, the officer who had been charged with bringing him into France provided him with some French currency for his expenses in Paris. He also advised him to change his clothes: a spy would guess immediately that he was on an important mission. He agreed to pass him off as an ordinary refugee who wanted to volunteer for the army.

Jan Karski followed his instructions. He took the train to Paris, then went to the recruitment camp of the Polish Army in Bessières, where he enrolled as a volunteer. From a phone booth, he called up Kulakowski, the private secretary of General Sikorski, the head of the government. Kulakowski told him to go to the Polish embassy, near Place des Invalides, where he would meet him and provide him with more funds. The Minister of the Interior, Stanislaw Kot, would be expecting him the next day in Angers, where the headquarters of the Polish government had been transferred.

Jan Karski took a hotel room on Boulevard Saint-Germain. It was now February 1940, and the time of the 'Phony War'. The café terraces were still packed and the atmosphere in Paris joyful.

The next day, he went to Angers. Kot was waiting for him in a restaurant. He was a small man with grey hair, who was extremely precise and rather pedantic. He sounded out Jan Karski, making him talk in great detail about himself and the other members of the Underground he knew. When Karski began to tell him the message from Warsaw, Kot told him to stop and write a report instead. He would provide him with a secretary and a typewriter. So, Jan Karski returned to Paris, where he spent the next six days drafting his report. This report, which was quite long, and which Jan Karski was to reconstitute from memory on several occasions, dwelled on the itinerary he had followed, the living conditions in countries under Nazi occupation, the currents of political opinion in Poland and the situation of the Jews in territories occupied by the Germans and the Soviets. As such, the Angers report was an abridged version of Jan Karski's book, and one of the first important testimonies dealing with the devastation of Europe, as well as the policy of terror aimed at the Jews, which was to lead to their destruction.

Jan Karski then managed to arrange a meeting with General Sikorski, who was considered in Poland to be a highly cultivated man, a democrat who, in the pre-war regime, had remained part of the opposition. After Poland's defeat during the *Blitzkrieg*, all the country's hopes had been pinned on him.

Wladislaw Sikorski was about sixty. He was courteous, energetic and extremely distinguished. He was already preparing for the post-war period. In his opinion, Poland should not just conduct a war of independence against Germany it should also fight to set up a genuinely democratic state. The Underground would play a vital role in this victory: in a sense, it was the Underground that would lead Poland towards democracy. For this reason, the head of the Polish government was in total agreement with the strategy of the leaders of the Underground, and with their desire to unify their organisations and turn them into a State.

Jan Karski went back to Poland using the same itinerary, but with different papers. A train took him to Budapest via Yugoslavia, where he was given a bag full of banknotes for the Polish Underground. Then he was driven to Kosice. Finally, the same guide as before led him through the mountains. But this was now April and the snow had melted. Jan Karski finished his journey on foot.

Once back in his country, Karski stayed for a while in Krakow. He noticed that the secret state had quickly come into being. He attended numerous discussions, concerning, for example, the choice of a government delegate to the Underground, or the setting-up of an Underground parliament.

Barely a month later, he was asked to go to France again, to inform the government of the decisions taken by the coalition. Each party made him swear an oath. As Karski puts it: 'I was sworn to transmit all the most important secrets, plans, internal affairs and points of view of *all four* of the political parties.'

In other words, he had become the courier of the secret Polish state.

It was now May 1940. Jan Karski took the same route via Zakopane in order to join his guide, and cross Slovakia with him until they reached Hungary.

He was carrying a microfilm of a thirty-eight-page message containing the plans for the organisation of the Underground. The film had not been developed and, if necessary, could be erased simply by exposing it to the light. This time, he was accompanied by a boy of seventeen, who wanted to volunteer for the Polish Army.

The situation was changing quickly in Europe. The Netherlands and Belgium had fallen. The Germans were now invading France. They were already advancing on Paris. Jan Karski realised that, if France was defeated, he would find himself in the middle of nowhere, with a seventeen-year-old boy in tow, because the defeat of France would lead to the collapse of the system of liaison between Poland and the government in exile.

The guide was worried: Franek, his predecessor, should have arrived a week ago, but had failed to appear, which was a bad sign. He thought it would be wise to postpone the journey. Jan Karski was against the idea. His mission was urgent. In any case, they had to wait for the weather to improve, and spent two days in a mountain chalet. The guide went down to the village to ask around. His sister, a girl of sixteen, was terrified: she was afraid that the Gestapo had arrested Franek. So the guide decided that the boy should remain in the chalet. He protested. He wanted to make his dream of joining the Polish Army come true. Jan Karski advised him against it. It was too dangerous.

It started to rain. Jan Karski and his guide decided to take advantage of the weather to start their journey, because according to the guide the border guards did not go out when it was raining. They thus managed to reach Slovakia, slithering through muddy forests every night and sleeping in damp caves. The rain kept up for three days. Jan Karski could not stand it anymore. His feet hurt. But the guide refused to stop in a village, because he believed that the Gestapo were watching the area. Jan Karski insisted. He was exhausted. On the edge of a village, they found a stream, where they washed and shaved so as not to attract attention. They dug a hole under a tree to hide their bags and took a room in an inn, where an old Slovak received them warmly.

All Jan Karski wanted to do was sleep. While the innkeeper brought them some liquor, sausages, bread and milk, Karski warmed himself up beside the stove. The guide asked about Franek. The innkeeper's answers were evasive. Jan Karski went to bed. He fell asleep at once, with the microfilm safe under his pillow. A few hours later, he was woken up by a cry and by a blow on his head. It was a rifle butt. Two Slovak policemen threw him out of the bed. He tried desperately to gather his wits. In a corner of the room, two other policemen—this time German— were sniggering. The guide was writhing in agony, his mouth bleeding. Jan Karski suddenly remembered the microfilm. He leapt onto the pillow, grabbed the roll and threw it into a bucket of water.

The policemen thought it was a grenade or a bomb. They drew back in panic. But as nothing happened, one of the Germans plunged a hand into the bucket and fished out the film. The other German started slapping Jan Karski, then shaking him. He wanted to know where his bag was, who he was with, and if he was hiding anything. Jan Karski did not reply, so the Germans started to beat him. They dragged him and the guide out of the inn. Then took them in opposite directions.

৵

Jan Karski was taken to the Slovak prison in Presov. In his cell, there was just a pail of water and a filthy straw mattress. He lay down on it. The guards in the corridor were Slovaks. Jan Karski wondered if the Gestapo were going to get on his case. Suddenly, two men burst in and threw themselves on him. One of them spat on his mattress. They took him away in a car to the police headquarters.

It was a small, smoky office. A red-haired man was sitting behind a square table, examining some papers. Soldiers in German uniforms were sitting along the walls, chatting and smoking cigarettes. Jan Karski was punched in the small of the back: 'Sit down, you dirty swine.' He stumbled and slumped onto the chair, facing the redhead, who was staring at him wearily, before pushing some papers towards him. 'Are these your papers?' he asked. Jan Karski panicked. He did not answer. He knew that, from this moment, the slightest mistake, or the slightest contradiction in what he said, would be fatal. The guard slapped him around to make him answer. Then he was asked what connection he had with the Underground movement. Jan Karski replied that he had nothing to do with any movement, and that he was the son of a teacher in Lwow, as his papers showed. The inspector adopted a sarcastic tone. He was sure that Jan Karski had carefully learned his part: 'And for how long have you been the son of a Lwow teacher? Two months...?Three months?'

The interrogation continued in this vein. The German soldiers seemed highly amused. The inspector was pleased to have an audience. It was clear that this was just the prelude, and that there was worse to come.

Jan Karski explained how he and his father had left their town to escape from the Soviets. He was a student, and the war had interrupted his studies, so he wanted to continue them in Switzerland. In Warsaw, a childhood friend of his had told him that he knew of a way to get to Geneva. He was ready to help him get as far as Kosice, in Hungary, if he gave a friend of his a film showing the ruins of Warsaw. Jan Karski had accepted, so his friend had given him the film, some money and the address of a guide who lived near the border.

The inspector listened to this tale with his eyes closed, his hands clasped behind his neck. When Jan Karski had finished, he slowly opened his eyes with a mocking smile.

He spoke to the man sitting next to him, who was writing non-stop: 'Did you get the touching story all down, Hans? I don't want a word changed. I want to read it exactly as it is.' Then he turned towards the guard: 'Get that lying bastard back to his cell.'

Jan Karski threw himself down onto the mattress. In his absence, a large spotlight had been installed, which produced an unbearable glare throughout the cell. His body, which had been tense during the interrogation, now relaxed, and he could not stop trembling. He had no illusions: the Germans had not believed his little story. But at least he did not have to invent anything anymore: he could now stick to that version. All night, phrases from his tale echoed round his mind.

At dawn, the guard came for him. They went to the same office as the day before. But the arrangement of the furniture had changed. There were now two tables, one large and the other small. Behind the small table was a typist. Behind the large one sat a huge Gestapo officer, who Jan Karski likens in his book to a seal. His fat seemed to have been moulded all in one piece. His face was bluish, with little dark eyes, a flat mouth and large flabby cheeks. Three other men were armed with clubs.

The Gestapo man's name was Pick—Inspector Pick. He

63

explained to Jan Karski that he never released anyone without first getting the truth out of them. Jan Karski was warned that he had to answer all of his questions without hesitation: he was not allowed to think first. If he did not cooperate, he would soon think of death as a luxury.

Pick started by asking him if he knew a man by the name of Franek, who had confessed everything: the route couriers took was now known to them down to the slightest detail. Jan Karski protested: 'I don't understand, I'm not a courier.' Pick gestured to the men standing behind Karski. At once, one of them struck him violently behind the ear with a club. The pain made Karski want to be sick. His head spun. He was going to vomit. Pick looked disgusted and told the men to get him out of there and take him to the bathroom. Jan Karski vomited into a stinking urinal. Then he was dragged back to his chair.

The interrogation continued. Inspector Pick asked him where his bag was, why he was in possession of a microfilm and why he had thrown it into a bucket of water. A guard broke one of his teeth when he hit him. Another blow came from a club. He collapsed to the floor and pretended to faint. The guards threw themselves onto him, pushed him up against the wall and beat him soundly. Then he really did pass out.

He was left to recover in his cell for three days. His body hurt everywhere and he could not even feed himself. On the second day, he was taken to a washroom so that he could remove the dried blood from his face. The Slovak soldiers were shaving. Jan Karski spotted a worn razor blade on the window ledge. He grabbed it, stuffed it in his pocket, then hid it in his mattress.

At the end of the third day, he was told that he would be questioned tomorrow by an SS officer. For this occasion, he was shaved and his clothes washed.

The SS was a *Junker* from Prussia. He was twenty-five, with a cold elegance. He had been trained from an early age at an *Ordensburg*, one of the schools where the Nazi elite were recruited. He asked the guards to leave, then started talking politely with Jan Karski, because he recognised that he was cultivated, or had 'breeding' as he puts it. 'If you were born a German,' he said, 'you would probably be very much like I am.'

They left the interrogation room for his personal office, which was furnished in mahogany, leather and velvet. There, the *Junker* officer offered Jan Karski a glass of brandy and a cigarette, confessing that he was bored of 'this Godforsaken hole of a Slovakian village'. He spoke to him about the virile principles of National Socialism, and expressed his great admiration for Baldur von Schirach, the head of the Nazi Youth, whom he found to be magnificent. He had been his favourite student at school. He blazed with enthusiasm for the coming *Pax Germanica* which, according to him, Hitler would proclaim on the steps of the White House in Washington. Then he suggested establishing contact between the Poles and the Germans: Jan Karski could be the special intermediary in this collaboration. 'If you love your country,' the SS officer said, 'you will not reject this proposition. It is your duty to give your leaders an opportunity to discuss the present situation with us.'

Jan Karski refused. The young officer's tone then changed completely. He now become fierce. He called the guard who, accompanied by two members of the Gestapo, brought him some photos. They were blow-ups of the film Karski had thrown into the water. The Germans had managed to save a part of it. The SS handed the pictures to Jan Karski, who took them with a trembling hand. He thought that the water would have destroyed the film. But the text was still perfectly legible, and was not even written in code.

The SS asked him if he recognised the text. Jan Karski said that there must have been a misunderstanding. He had been deceived, because he did not know this text at all. The SS was furious. He grabbed a riding crop and struck Karski's cheek. The Gestapo officers then threw themselves on Jan Karski again, punching him violently.

When he was put back in his cell, Jan Karski lay on his mattress. He couldn't take any more. He writes how his face, covered in blood and puffy, had nothing human left about it. He had lost four of his teeth. He was in excruciating pain all over, and would not survive another session like that. So he decided to put an end to it all. He slit his left wrist with the razor blade, but failed to reach the vein. He tried again, harder. The blood spurted out like a fountain. Then he cut his other wrist. He lay down, his arms stretched alongside his body, his blood forming a pool. Within a few minutes, he began to feel weak. His blood had stopped flowing. So he waved his arms in the air to make the bleeding start again. The blood burst out in a rush. Jan Karski started to choke. He tried to breath through his mouth. He retched, vomited, then passed out.

꿈

He woke up in the Slovakian hospital of Preszow. He immediately thought of the possibility of making another suicide attempt, or of escaping. A Slovak policeman was sitting in the corridor, just beside the door. Jan Karski slumped into a stupor, and fell back to sleep in despair.

The next day, a nun was standing over him, holding a thermometer. Slovakian is similar to Polish, and Jan Karski understood that she was trying to encourage him: 'It's better to be here than in prison. We will try to keep you here as long as possible.'

He stayed in bed for a week. It was impossible to use his hands. Splints were keeping his wrists in place. 'The days I spent in that Slovakian hospital in Preszow were perhaps the strangest of my life,' he writes. Oddly enough, this rest made him feel exulted in a way he had never felt before: his body was recovering its strength. But, at the same time, he had fits of depression and was terrorised by the idea that he would soon be back in the Gestapo's hands.

On the fifth day, he asked the nun for a newspaper. The headline, in huge black letters, hit him like a bomb exploding in his face: '*France Surrenders!*' The article explained how France had admitted defeat, and there was even talk of collaboration with Germany. 'We had based the hope for Poland's freedom on a French victory,' Jan Karski says. 'Now I could see no hope.'

On the seventh day, two Gestapo officers burst into his room. They wanted to take Jan Karski away. A doctor intervened, and whispered into Jan Karski's ear: 'Act as sick as you can. I'll telephone.'

Karski staggered through the hospital, supported by the two Gestapo men. Once outside, he stumbled and almost collapsed. He was pushed into a car to be taken to the prison. When they arrived, he was dragged to the interrogation room. He tripped on purpose and fell over. He was taken to his cell, where he fell asleep. A few hours later, the prison doctor examined him. He was a Slovak, and had received a phone call from his colleague at the hospital. He now ordered them to take him back. The two Gestapo men were furious, but drove him to the hospital.

Jan Karski spent his time dozing. He was at a dead end: forced to simulate illness to protect himself from the Gestapo, but with no way out.

One day, a girl visited him. She gave him a bunch of roses. She spoke German and asked Karski to forgive her people. Was it a trap? Jan Karski had never seen her before. The guard grabbed her, tearing her bouquet to shreds in search of a message, then dragged her out of the room. Then another Gestapo officer arrived, claiming that using a bearer of roses was a ridiculous strategy, but since Jan Karski's friends now knew where he was, they would have to transfer him.

He was driven away in a car again. They drove for a long time, one village after another passed by. All Karski could think of was committing suicide. Then, suddenly, he recognised where he was: in southern Poland. They had arrived in a small town where he had carried out several missions. He could not believe his eyes, because he actually had many contacts in the area. The car stopped in front of the hospital. His bandages were soaked in blood. He was carried to a bed on the third floor. Jan Karski wondered if this was some new ordeal that the Germans had dreamed up. Had they taken him to this town to act as a lure for his comrades? Yet, he found it impossible to believe that they had located his contacts.

A doctor arrived, watched by the Gestapo officer. He was Polish and whispered words of encouragement while he was examining him. 'Shall I let someone know about you?' he asked. Once again, Jan Karski thought this must be a trap. But the doctor reassured him: the entire staff of the hospital was Polish, and there was not a single traitor among them. A nun took his temperature, and falsified the result by raising it considerably. To protect him from the Nazis, the doctor in charge declared that Jan Karski was in a critical condition. While the guard's attention was being distracted, he whispered to Jan Karski to simulate a nervous fit and then ask for a priest. So Karski started twitching. He shook convulsively, saying that he was going to die and that he wanted to confess. A wheelchair was brought and, under the surveillance of the Nazi guard, the nun pushed him to the chapel, where an old priest listened to his confession with a great deal of interest. Jan Karski continued to act as if he were at death's door. He was given permission to return to the chapel every day. A nun prayed by his side. He took the risk of asking her to go into town and tell a certain Stefi that he was here: 'Tell her Witold sent you.' (Witold was his pseudonym in the Underground.) The next day, she told him that a nun from a neighbouring convent was going to visit him. He realised that this was a message, and that a plan must already be in preparation.

Three days later, the 'nun' arrived. Jan Karski recognised the young sister of the guide who had been arrested with him. She whispered to him that the leaders knew everything that had happened, and that he would have to wait a little longer. Karski asked for news of her brother. With tears in her eyes, she said: 'We haven't heard from him.'

Jan Karski explained to her that the Gestapo must have brought him here to make him betray his comrades. He could not stand any more torture. He needed some poison.

She came back five days later: 'They know everything. You have been awarded the Cross of Valor.' She slipped him a cyanide pill.

That very evening, the doctor told him that he was going to be freed during the night. There was nothing to fear from the guard, who had been bribed. At midnight, the doctor would come into the room and light a cigarette. That was the signal. Karski would then have to go down to the first floor. He would find a rose on a sill, he should jump from that window and some men below would catch him.

At midnight, he slipped out of bed with his cyanide pill, ready to swallow it if he felt in any danger. He went downstairs completely naked. A window was open. On the floor, there was a rose, which the wind had just blown off. He climbed onto the window ledge and looked down. A voice said: 'Hurry, we haven't a moment to lose!' He jumped. Hands grabbed him forcefully before he hit the ground. He was given some pants and a shirt, then the men ran with him to the railings. They were barefoot, too. They helped him over the fence, then continued to run through the fields. Jan Karski stumbled and fell. One of his comrades hauled him over his shoulder and carried him through the woods. A river glittered in the darkness. There was a whistle, then two armed men emerged from the undergrowth. They exchanged a few words, then moved off. The journey continued along the riverbank, until another figure appeared, a childhood friend of Karski's called Staszeck Rosa, who was a young socialist.

A canoe had been concealed among the reeds. They got into it and cast off from the bank. There were five of them in the boat and the rower had problems steering it. The boat swayed and Karski fell overboard. They dragged him back aboard and he lay down, shivering. At last they reached the other side. Rosa hid the canoe in the gorse. Another hour's march through the forest. There was a village in the distance, and a barn. They split up. The barn was for Jan Karski.

He tried to thank Rosa, who told him with a mocking grin that if the mission had failed, he had been told to shoot him. 'Be grateful to the Polish workers,' he added. 'They saved you.'

ಲ

Jan Karski spent three days hidden in the barn. He hardly ate, suffered from trembling fits and could not sleep. The Gestapo were looking for him, the roads were being watched and the vehicles checked. A messenger informed him that he would soon leave for a small property in the mountains, where he would stay for at least four months. The Gestapo had to lose all trace of him. There was also the fact that anyone who had been in the hands of the Germans, like him, had to be kept away from their own leaders. That was the rule. They were treated as suspects and isolation was essential.

An old cart arrived to fetch him at dawn. Jan Karski was hidden in a barrel covered with straw. He had to hunch up inside it, his chin on his knees and his arms round his legs. Towards noon, the cart came to a halt. He emerged from his hiding place. They were in a forest, and he was happy to be able to breathe freely. He stretched—everything seemed soft, green and fresh.

A girl was waiting for him beside a car. Jan Karski noticed her 'slender, lithe figure, the freshness of her skin, and her general air of grace'. He adds that he found her 'attractive'. Her name was Danuta Sawa, and she was Walentyna Sawa's daughter. 'We live on an estate nearby,' she said.

Jan Karski was to have a new identity. In the Underground, the set of information required to make up a biography was called a 'legend'. And it was Danuta who had been instructed to provide him with his new legend: she told him, rather cheekily, that from now on he was her cousin—a cousin who had just arrived from Krakow, a rather idle sort of ne'er-do-well, who did not really have to work for a living. He had fallen ill and his doctor had advised rest in the countryside. He had been trained as an agronomist, and so could help the day labourers in the garden.

Amused, Jan Karski protested that he knew nothing about gardening. Danuta reminded him that he was supposed to be lazy: that way he could spend his time doing nothing.

He explored the estate, made up of a manor house, which sparkled white in the sunlight like something out of a novel, with its stables and outhouses, and an immense garden planted with beeches, which also contained the farm buildings. The Underground, the Gestapo, his escape...everything seemed so far away now to Jan Karski.

He spent three weeks recuperating. He stayed in bed and lazed about. To keep up the deception, he would inspect the estate from time to time, coming out with some botanical remarks, which he had learned by heart. He saddled a horse and went riding. At night, from his window, he noticed Danuta in the garden with a man. It was her brother, Lucjan, who was in the Underground. He used to meet his sister in secret.

Jan Karski was soon bored. He wanted to start working again for the Underground, and asked Lucjan for something to do. He requested the agreement of the leaders, who gave him the task of producing propaganda. So Jan Karski wrote appeals to the Polish people aimed at galvanising their spirit of resistance. He drafted all sorts of pamphlets, proclamations and even periodicals. Lucjan's sudden arrest by the Gestapo made Jan Karski's immediate departure necessary. He left the manor, and never saw Danuta again.

≈

He resumed service in Krakow. For seven months, from February to September 1941, the Underground made use of his knowledge of foreign languages. He was asked to listen to all sorts of radio broadcasts and to write a report for the Underground leaders every day. During this period, many networks were being dismantled by the Nazis, and several vital leaders had been arrested. But it was also at this time that the Polish Underground was being reorganised on a larger scale. It had taken the form which had been desired for it by the leaders of the movement and General Sikorski right from the start: it was now like a genuine State, with an administrative wing, an armed wing (the *Armia Krajowa*), a parliamentary wing and a judicial wing, which would see to it that Poland would be freed of traitors and collaborators. Thus, from that moment onwards, its structure became extremely complex and opaque, even for its members: those who were arrested by the Gestapo and thought that the central authorities would be in danger—because the Germans had questioned them about one or two names they thought were important—generally did not realise that these were merely the leaders of their own little group.

At this point in his book, Jan Karski deplores the fact that the sacrifices of the Polish people had not been recognised by the entire world. In several instances, he displays a certain bitterness and a feeling of injustice: the Allies did not react when his country was dismantled, nor did they react, five years later, during the Warsaw Uprising, when they left the Poles to be massacred. He reminds us that, in terms of democracy, Poland has no lessons to be learnt from anyone: its government did not collaborate with the Nazi occupiers, as was the case in other countries. Jan Karski writes tactfully, and merely suggests the idea, but it would seem that in his eyes, and in the eyes of the Polish people, Poland was abandoned and this will always be so. Abandoned by Europe, abandoned by History, abandoned by the world's memory.

❧

Around the month of April, he received an order to change addresses: a woman who lived in the same building had been arrested. Jan Karski did not know her, but the Underground decided that he should flee. A few nights after moving, he heard that two members of the Gestapo had come asking for him at his former address. So he began living at several addresses at once. He continued listening to the radio. In order to remain unnoticed, he also found a job as an assistant in a bookstore. His radio was kept in the bedroom of an old lady's apartment. One of the houses where he slept was a cooperative, run by a certain Tadeusz Kielec, a brilliant, colourful figure, whom Karski had known since high school. Neither of them revealed their identities or questioned the other, but, as Jan Karski noticed, once you have worked undercover, it is possible to spot everyone else who is also undercover. Kielec was arrested near Lublin when he tried to derail a convoy of weapons from the USSR with three of his men. Kielec ran a small independent unit. He and his men were hanged in public on the market square in Lublin and their bodies left on the gallows for two days as an example to the population.

After Kielec's arrest, the Gestapo searched the cooperative. When Jan Karski was warned, the Germans were just three doors away from his room. He managed to escape all the same, but without being able to take anything with him.

It was a difficult period. He had run out of money. It was impossible to get new identity papers. He then made the acquaintance of Weronika Laskowa, a beautiful forty-year-old, who took him in. She was married to a former diplomat who had joined the free Polish Army abroad. To survive, she served meals in her large dining room, which attracted a great many people. Members of the Underground took advantage of the crush there to meet up. Among them was Cyna, the head of the Socialist networks, to whom Jan Karski owed his escape, and Kara, the commander of the armed forces in the region. Jan Karski then started working in the press office of a military unit, and was in permanent contact with these two men.

As Jan Karski himself points out, even though people may imagine that life in the Underground must be continually full of thrilling mysteries, most of the time their lives were 'wholly devoid of sensational exploits'. In fact, a war of information required patient office work: in this case, it meant putting together a press dossier of all the Underground publications for the authorities, and above all for the government which, after the Nazi invasion of France, had been transferred to London.

Around Easter time, there was a flurry of arrests. Their equipment was seized on a number of occasions. One day, Cyna arrived in Weronika Laskowa's apartment looking very worried. He had made an appointment with Kara, who had not shown up. He decided to go to his house. Everyone advised him against it, but he went anyway. 'Cyna never came back,' Jan Karski wrote.

He and Weronika Laskowa packed their things into a suitcase and left. Nowhere was safe anymore and they did not want to compromise their friends. For several hours, they wandered through the streets of Krakow, then put their suitcase in the left-luggage office at the train station and took a room in a hotel used by prostitutes (they knew that no one would look for them there).

Some days later, Jan Karski re-established contact with the organisation. He learned what had happened. It had all started with the arrest of a liaison agent who, under torture, had revealed the addresses of certain meeting places. So the Nazis had been able to start watching the network which Jan Karski was part of, but without arresting anybody. They soon discovered where Kara lived. They arrested him at home, then waited for all those who had appointments with him to come to his house, one by one. In this way, four members had fallen into the trap, including Cyna.

The organisation did all it could to rescue Kara and Cyna from prison, but the Gestapo realised that they had captured some important people, and watched over them closely. There was no news of Cyna for a long time, but a message did reach them from Kara: he could no longer bear what he was suffering and wanted some poison. The leadership of the Underground sent him two cyanide pills, with this message: 'You have been decorated with the order of *Virtuti Militari*. Cyanide enclosed. We will meet some time, Brother.'

The next day, Kara was buried in the prison courtyard. As for Cyna, they learned a few months later that he had been sent to Auschwitz.

The Underground forces of the region were totally reorganised. Addresses, contact points and hideouts were all modified. Weronika Laskowa went back to her apartment. Jan Karski was transferred to Warsaw, where he took control of a liaison unit between the political leaders of the Underground.

&

In Warsaw, Jan Karski frequently saw his bother Marian who, before the war, used to be a police chief. He had been sent to Auschwitz-I in 1940, but had managed to escape and now held a key post in the Underground movement. He told Jan Karski about his detention in 'one of the worst concentration camps in all Europe'. What his brother told him 'outdid in horror nearly everything that I had ever heard.'

During this period, Jan Karski was sometimes sent on missions, to Lublin for example, to pass on information. He would then take the train, with his radio bulletins and all kinds of secret reports; his technique was not at all to conceal them, but instead to hold them under his arm, wrapped up in a newspaper like a loaf of bread.

Above all, his work meant that he was in contact with a large number of leaders of the organisation, whose various needs and decisions he relayed to the others. He thus occupied a strategic position, which allowed him to become familiar with the structures of the Underground, and to understand better the situation in Poland.

Like everyone else who lived in Warsaw at the time, Jan Karski witnessed the infamy of the Germans, whose repressive machine was now making daily life in Poland unlivable. Schools were closed and teaching forbidden. A famine program maintained the population under the bread line. Polish newborn babies were systematically deported ('No one is even sure of exactly what did happen to them,' Jan Karski notes demurely).

❧

It was during the summer of 1942 that he was given a new mission as a courier of the Polish government in exile in London. He acquired a new identity from one of the French workers whom the Vichy regime lent to the Germans, as part of their state collaboration, so they could do jobs in Poland. These workers were granted two weeks' leave every three months to see their families in France. One of them sold his papers to Jan Karski, at a high price, so that he could go in his place. The agreement was simple: the man who had sold his identity would go on holiday to a beautiful estate which would be lent to him in the countryside (in this case, near Lublin). Two weeks later, he would reappear and claim that his papers had been stolen from him in a tram.

A few days before leaving, Jan Karski was informed that he was going to see the Executive Committee of the political wing—in other words, the Underground parliament. The meeting took place in an apartment, which was reached via a labyrinthine route, whose entrance lay under a church.

'As I entered,' writes Jan Karski, 'I saw grouped around the table the men who controlled the destiny of Poland.' They included the delegate of the government in exile, the Commander in Chief of the Home Army, the director of the government delegation, as well as representatives of the main political parties. Jan Karski was welcomed warmly. General Grot joked with him: 'Are you really willing to go? Last time you took a trip we had a devil of a time getting you away from the Gestapo.'

The delegate opened the session. He informed his colleagues that the objective of the committee meeting—the thirty-second one—was to deliver to the courier Witold documents for their government in London and for the leaders of the political parties concerning the situation in Poland and their Underground activities. Jan Karski would also enter into contact with the Allied authorities.

The documents that Jan Karski had to take to England comprised about a thousand pages on a microfilm concealed in the handle of a razor. In code, there were also the minutes of their meeting, which would be the basis of Jan Karski's report in London. A coded message was sent to England, as well as the organisation in France: 'Karski leaving soon. Goes through Germany, Belgium, France, Spain. Two-week stay in France, two weeks in Spain. Inform all "transfer cells" in France, also all Allied representatives in Spain. Password: "Coming to see Aunt Sophie." Announce him as Karski.'

❧

It was the end of August. Before he left, a meeting was arranged with two leaders of the Jewish Underground. One represented the Zionists, the other the Jewish Socialist Alliance, or Bund.

They met in a ruined house. The two men had overcome their political differences: what they wanted to tell Jan Karski, and through him the Polish and Allied governments, came from the entirety of the Jewish population.

'What I learned at the meetings we held in that house,' Jan Karski writes, 'and later, when I was taken to see the facts for myself, was horrible, beyond description.' According to him, nothing comparable had ever occurred in the history of humanity.

The two men lived outside the ghetto but could go there at will, because they had found a way to visit it whenever they wanted. Jan Karski noted that the leader of the Bund would pass 'easily as a Polish nobleman'; he was an elegant sixty-year-old, with bright eyes and a large moustache. The Zionist was younger: he was about forty and very nervy; he could scarcely control himself.

Immediately, Jan Karski realised that their situation was totally desperate: 'You other Poles are fortunate,' the Zionist leader said. 'From this ocean of tears, pain, rage and humiliation your country will re-emerge, but the Polish Jews will no longer exist.'

The Zionist thought that the Poles were lucky: despite their suffering, despite the extent of their tragedy, their nation would survive, their towns would be rebuilt and Poland would exist once more. There would be victory for the Allies, but not for the Jews: 'The Jewish people will be murdered.'

Jan Karski was sitting on a broken chair, its legs propped up on bricks. The two men were pacing around the room. Karski noticed how their shadows danced in the candlelight.

He did not move. He was petrified by what he was hearing.

The Zionist broke down; he started sobbing: what was the good of talking? This extermination was incomprehensible; he himself did not understand it.

Jan Karski would help them. He would give a report in London. He said he would speak about the fate of the Jews.

'We want you to tell the Polish and Allied governments,' the Bund leader said, 'that we are helpless in the face of the German criminals. We cannot defend ourselves and no one in Poland can defend us. The Polish Underground authorities can save some of us but they cannot save masses. The Germans are not trying to enslave us as they have other people; we are being systematically murdered.'

'That is what people do not understand,' the Zionist added. 'That is what is so difficult to make clear.'

Jan Karski writes: 'This was the solemn message I carried to the world.'

The two men had prepared a detailed report for him. Jan Karski wanted precise information. He asked how many Jews in the ghetto were already dead. 'The exact figure can be very nearly computed from the German deportation orders,' the Zionist replied. Jan Karski was surprised: all of those deported had been killed? 'Every single one,' the Bund leader confirmed.

He added that the Germans were still telling lies about the matter, but no doubts now remained. All those who were taken by train from the ghetto went directly to the death camps.

They told Jan Karski that the initial orders had arrived in July, just two months previously. The Germans had requested five thousand people per day from the Jewish Council in the ghetto, supposedly to go and work outside Warsaw. The number had then gone up on a daily basis, and when it had reached ten thousand, Czerniakow, the director of the Council, had committed suicide.

'In two and a half months, in one district in Poland, the Nazis had committed three hundred thousand murders,' Jan Karski writes.

The two men then suggested that Jan Karski go with them to the ghetto. 'As an eyewitness I would be more convincing than a mere mouthpiece.' Jan Karski was warned that, if he accepted, not only would he risk his life, but he would also remain haunted by what he would see.

Jan Karski accepted. The second meeting took place in the same ruined house. It was devoted to preparing his visit to the ghetto. Then Jan Karski went back over the message he was to relay for them to London. What should he say if he were asked: 'How can we help?'

The Zionist replied that they should bomb German cities, and inform the Germans of the Jews' fate by using leaflets. They should threaten the entire German nation with a similar destiny if the atrocities were not stopped at once.

The Bund leader was well aware that such a plan did not enter into the Allies' military strategy. But neither the Jews nor anyone willing to help them could now consider this war in purely military terms. They had to convince the Allied governments to declare officially to the Germans that their continued extermination of the Jews would lead to terrible reprisals: that Germany would be totally destroyed.

Jan Karski said that he would do his best to make people understand this position.

'It is an unprecedented situation in history,' the Zionist said, 'and can be dealt with only with unprecedented methods. Let the Allied governments...begin public executions of Germans, any they can get hold of.'

Jan Karski protested: such a demand would only horrify the Allies.

Both men realised that, but it was still necessary. They were calling for this so that the world would at last understand what was happening to them. So that the world would know how alone and defenceless they were. The Allies would win the war by the following year, or maybe two years at most, but that would do nothing for the Jews, because they would no longer exist. How was it possible that Western democracies were allowing them to die like that? Why didn't they try to organise a mass escape? Why didn't they offer money to the Germans? Why were the lives of Polish Jews not being redeemed?

Both men were extremely agitated. They started to get carried away. When Jan Karski asked them what action plan should be suggested to the Jewish leaders in Britain and America, the Bund leader gripped his arm so violently that it hurt.

He yelled at Jan Karski that there was now no longer any place for politics or diplomacy: 'Tell them that the earth must be shaken to its foundations, the world must be aroused.' In his opinion, the Allies had to find unheard-of means of hitting back, because a purely military victory would not stop the German program of destruction. The Jewish leaders in Britain and America should contact as many influential people and institutions as possible and demand action to save the Jewish people. They should be prepared to do anything in order to get their agreement. They should go on hunger strikes. If necessary, they should let themselves die in front of the entire world. 'This may shake the conscience of the world,' the Bund leader said.

Jan Karski could not take any more. He writes how, by then, he was in a cold sweat. He wanted to get to his feet.

But they had one more thing to tell him: the Warsaw ghetto was going to declare war on Germany: 'the most desperate declaration of war that has ever been made,' they said. It was out of the question for them to be massacred without fighting back. They were waiting for arms from the *Armia Krajowa*, and had started organising the defence of the ghetto. They were under no illusions about their chances of success, but they wanted the entire world to know about their fight—for its desperate character to be recognised, 'as a demonstration and a reproach,' they said.

ॐ

Two days later, Jan Karski went into the Warsaw ghetto. His guide was the Bund leader. There was also a third man, whom Karski describes simply as being 'another of the Jewish Underground'. The streets had been devastated and the houses ruined. A brick wall and barbed wire ringed off the area where the Jews were imprisoned. Jan Karski and his two companions went in through a 'secret passage', used by the Underground: it lay in a house on Muranowska Street, whose front door led out to the exterior of the ghetto, and whose basement led inside. 'This building,' writes Jan Karski, 'had become like a modern version of the river Styx which connected the world of the living with the world of the dead.'

Jan Karski wrote his book in 1944. As his two informants had told him, there had been an uprising in the Warsaw ghetto a year before. He thus felt free to talk about that house and basement without endangering anyone.

The men and women Jan Karski saw inside the ghetto were still alive but, as he put it, 'there was nothing human left in these palpitating figures'. Was it possible for a man to be still alive and yet no longer human? This was the threshold that Jan Karski encountered during his visit—and it was a threshold that would obsess him. He writes: 'As we picked our way across the mud and rubble, the shadows of what had once been men or women flitted by us.'

Everywhere, there was hunger, groaning children, stinking corpses. All around, starving gazes. A group of men, escorted by police, were marching by in step, like robots. An old man was leaning against a wall, his body shaking.

Children were playing in a park. 'They play before they die,' the guide told him, with no sign of emotion. Jan Karski replied that these children were not playing, it was just make-believe play.

Corpses were lying naked on the street. Why, Karski asked, were they lying there naked? The guide then explained that, when a Jew died, they removed his clothes and threw his body out onto the street. They would have to pay to have him buried and, here, no one could pay. And it meant that they could get his clothes back. 'Here, every rag counts,' the guide said.

Suddenly, his two companions grabbed him by the arm and dragged him towards a door. Jan Karski was afraid. He thought that he had been recognised. 'Hurry, hurry, you must see this. This is something for you to tell the world about!'

They climbed up to the top floor. They heard a gunshot.

They knocked on doors, searching for a window that looked out over the street. Finally, they were let into an apartment. Jan Karski was pushed over to the window and told to look: 'Now you'll see something. The hunt.'

In the middle of the street were two teenagers in Hitler Youth uniform. Their blond hair shone in the sunlight, Karski observes. They had round faces, pink cheeks and were chatting merrily. Abruptly, the younger one drew a revolver from his pocket. 'He was looking for a target,' Jan Karski writes, 'with the casual, gay absorption of a boy at a carnival.' The boy's gaze came to rest on a spot that lay outside Jan Karski's range of vision. He raised his arm, aimed, and they heard a shot, followed by breaking glass and a man's cry. The boy was delighted, and the second one congratulated him. They then continued on their way.

Jan Karski was paralysed, his 'face glued to the window', as he puts it. He had the impression that if he moved, something similar would happen to him. He felt a hand on his shoulder. It was a woman, the apartment's tenant: 'Go back,' she told him. 'Run away. Don't torture yourself any more.'

Karski's two companions were sitting on a bed, over-whelmed, their heads in their hands. He asked them to take him back. He could not stand any more. He had to leave.

The three of them went down into the street without saying a word. Once downstairs, Karski almost broke into a run, until they were outside the ghetto.

He came back two days later. This time, his description of his visit is just one sentence long. He writes: 'With my two guides

I walked again for three hours through the streets of this inferno, the better to testify the truth.'

⤨

Jan Karski now breaks his chronology. He immediately adds, without even changing paragraphs, that he described his impressions to 'members of the British and American governments, and to the Jewish leaders of both continents'. He did what he could: 'I told what I had seen in the ghetto.' Among others, he told certain writers—H.G. Wells and Arthur Koestler—'as they could describe it with greater force and talent than I.'

Then, just as abruptly, he starts recounting one of these interviews in London. It was with Szmul Zygielbojm, the Bund's representative on the National Council of the Polish government in exile.

Szmul Zygielbojm was one of those remarkable men who become completely devoted to the cause they are defending. He had already tried to alert the world about the extermination of the Jews, by reading on the radio a message that described the Chelmno massacre, when several hundreds of thousands of Polish Jews were gassed in trucks.

A meeting was arranged on 2 December 1942, at Stratton House, near Piccadilly, at the headquarters of the Polish Ministry of the Interior. Jan Karski had already been in London for five weeks, his time completely taken up by talks, meetings and interviews. He was exhausted.

Zygielbojm was about forty, with a piercing stare and the sort of intensity that sometimes comes from extreme fatigue.

'What do you want to hear about?' Karski asked him, rather brusquely.

Zygielbojm replied, with a sort of despairing calm, that he wanted to know everything about the Jews. He told him that he, too, was Jewish. He asked Karski to tell him everything he knew.

Jan Karski told Szmul Zygielbojm about his meeting with the two Jewish leaders in the ruined house, then his two visits to the ghetto. Zygielbojm listened to him extremely attentively, his eyes wide open. He asked for all sorts of details, wanting to know the exact words of the woman who had laid her hand on Jan Karski's shoulder, or more details about the houses, the children and the corpses lying on the streets.

At the end of the interview, Zygielbojm was exhausted. 'His eyes,' Jan Karski noted, 'were nearly starting out of their sockets.' He promised to do everything he could.

A few months later, on May 13 1943, Jan Karski heard that Szmul Zygielbojm, member of the National Polish Council and representative of the Bund in London, had committed suicide. He had left a note saying that he had done everything in his power to help the Jews in Poland, but had failed, that his brothers had perished, and now he would join them. He had gassed himself.

૭

Back to chronology. A few days after his second visit to the Warsaw ghetto, the Bund leader who had acted as his guide suggested showing Jan Karski 'a Jewish death camp'. This is one of the most contested passages of the book; some even think that

Jan Karski could not possibly have seen what he described.

The camp was near the town of Belzec, a hundred miles east of Warsaw. Karski provided no other information, but the site has since been identified as the camp of Izbica Lubelska.

A large number of Estonians, Lithuanians and Ukrainians, who were employed there as prison guards, had spoken to Jewish organisations in return for money. One of these guards, a Ukrainian, lent Jan Karski his papers and uniform one day when he was on leave. There was so much disorder and corruption in the camp that he was told he would not be noticed. For greater safety, a second Ukrainian accompanied him. On their way to the camp, he explained to Jan Karski that the gate they had to pass through was guarded by Germans. They never checked the Ukrainian guards' papers; they just had to salute and greet them.

The camp was on a plain, surrounded by barbed wire. It was watched over by a large number of armed guards. Meanwhile, outside, one patrol followed another at a distance of fifty yards. There were cries, gunshots, and a terrible stench. The area between the buildings was covered by 'a dense, pulsating, throbbing, noisy human mass'—'insane human beings in constant, agitated motion', as Jan Karski writes. To the left of the entrance, there was a railway track, or rather a 'raised passage', as he specifies. An old freight train of about thirty wagons was stationary. 'That's the train they'll load them on,' said the guard. 'You'll see it all.'

They went through the gate, where two German non-commissioned officers saluted them off-handedly.

'The chaos, the squalor, the hideousness of it all was simply indescribable,' Jan Karski writes. An old man was sitting, naked, on the ground. Beside him was a child in rags, who was staring around in fright, his body shaken by spasms. The buildings were full, so those who had failed to find room inside crouched outside in the cold. Thousands of men and women were there, trembling, screaming, clasping onto one another. They were terrorised, and dying of hunger, thirst and exhaustion. Most of them had lost all control of themselves and were acting like mad people. 'They had become,' Karski writes, 'at this stage, completely dehumanized.'

The guard explained that they all came from the ghettos. They had been left in the camp for four days without the slightest drop of water or food. Those who had brought anything with them in the train had been robbed by the Germans.

They had to cross the entire camp to reach the point which the guard had selected for Jan Karski. To do so, they were forced to walk across piles of bodies. Jan Karski was gripped by nausea and stopped, but his guide pulled him forwards.

They arrived at a position about twenty yards away from the gate through which the Jews were going to be pushed into the wagons. This was a good spot, the Ukrainian told him. He asked Jan Karski not to move. From there, he would see what was going to happen next.

'At each moment I felt the impulse to run,' he writes. 'I had to force myself to remain indifferent, practise stratagems on myself to convince myself that I was not one of the condemned.' An SS officer started barking out orders, asking for the gate to be opened. It led directly to the freight train wagons, which were blocking the way. The SS turned around towards the crowd and, hands on hips, announced that all the Jews were to get onto the train, which would take them away to a place where they would work. Suddenly, with a loud laugh, he produced a revolver and fired into the crowd. A cry was heard. He put his gun back into his holster and yelled: '*Alle Jüden, raus, raus.*' Gunshots were now coming from all sides. In a panic, the crowd rushed towards the narrow passage through the gateway and quickly filled up two of the wagons. The Germans crammed them inside with blows from the butts of their guns. The wagons were now full, but they continued. 'These unfortunates,' Jan Karski writes, 'crazed by what they had been through...began to climb on the heads and shoulders of those in the trains...They were helpless and responded only with howls to those who, clutching at their hair and clothes for support, trampled on necks, faces and shoulders, breaking bones and shouting with insensate fury.'

At last, the guards pulled closed the doors and bolted them with iron bars.

The scene that Jan Karski then recounts has given rise to a number of questions. He himself, when he wrote his book, was aware of this possibility: 'I know that many people will not believe me,' he writes, 'will think that I exaggerate or invent. But I saw it and it is not exaggerated or invented. I have no other proof, no photographs. All I can say is that I saw it and that it is the truth.'

The floor of the train, he explained, had been covered with quicklime. With the heat inside the wagons, the bodies became wet; they then dehydrated on contact with the quicklime and burned. 'The occupants of the cars would be literally burnt to death before long, their flesh eaten from their bones,' Jan Karski writes.

It took the Germans three hours to fill up the train. Night had fallen when the last wagon was closed. Jan Karski had counted: there were forty-six of them. He heard screams from inside. And, in the camp, dozens of people lay dying on the ground. The German policemen finished them off.

The train pulled away. Jan Karski did not know where it went, but, according to his 'informants', it would continue for about eighty miles, then stop in the middle of the countryside and wait there for several days, 'while death penetrated into every corner of its interior.' It is more likely that the train stopped on the ramp of the Belzec death camp. Because, as Jan Karski points out, the Jews were then charged with cleaning the wagons, taking out the corpses and throwing them into a mass grave. Meanwhile, as he indicates, the Izbica Lubelska camp, where he was standing, would be filled up once more. The train would come back empty, and it would start all over again.

Jan Karski and his guide left the camp without any difficulty. They separated. Jan Karski returned the uniform he had been lent. He washed himself repeatedly, then lay down under a tree and fell asleep. On waking, he was gripped by terrible nausea, and vomited a red liquid constantly all day. Then he fell back to sleep for thirty-six hours. Finally, he was helped onto the train to Warsaw.

'The images of what I saw in the death camp are, I am afraid, my permanent possessions,' he writes. 'I would like nothing better than to purge my mind of these memories. For one thing, the recollection of these events invariably brings on a recurrence of the nausea. But more than that, I would like simply to be free of them, to obliterate the very thought that such things occurred.'

It was now September 11 1942, and Jan Karski left Poland. He took the train to Berlin. As he had French papers, he tried not to speak too much, to avoid being unmasked. He pretended to have a toothache and, during the entire journey, he dabbed at his mouth with a handkerchief.

His mission was now to reach England, with his microfilm concealed in the handle of his razor. A mass had been held for him a few days before his departure, in the presence of his best friends, who presented him with a communion wafer, which Jan Karski was then to carry around his neck in a locket during this journey across occupied Europe.

In Berlin, Jan Karski had a little time on his hands. As he wanted to discover more about the real situation in Germany, he paid a visit to his old friend, Rudolf Strauch. In the days he had spent studying in Europe's universities, before the war, he had frequented the Staatsbibliothek in Berlin. At that time, he had lodged with the Strauch family, who had liked his liberal, democratic ideas.

The Strauchs had changed completely. Jan Karski's visit created a malaise. They had now become fervent Hitler supporters and Jan Karski was obliged to pretend that he too backed the regime. They went out for dinner to a restaurant off Unter den Linden avenue. There, his friend, who was afraid of being seen with a foreigner, finally told him that all the

Poles were Hitler's enemies and they could not see each other anymore.

Jan Karski left the restaurant at once, suspecting that his former friends had alerted the police, and, in a fury, took refuge in the waiting-room at the station, until it was time to take the train to Brussels.

He then changed trains to Paris where, in a confectionery shop near the Gare du Nord, he gave his password to an old woman, who put him in contact with some Polish officers in the Underground movement. They provided him with a new passport. He then stayed for a few days in Lyon, where he prepared his journey to Spain. After that, he left for Perpignan, where a young Spanish couple were to find him a guide. The border was closely watched, and they had to wait. In the end, a certain Fernando agreed to take him across. They went on bicycle, at night. Fernando led the way, Jan Karski following at a distance of about fifty yards, with his lights off. It was agreed that if Fernando stopped and rang his bell, then Jan Karski should hide. Half an hour later, the bell rang. Jan Karski turned back. There was a German patrol. The next day, they tried again. This time he and Fernando started out on foot, and then continued by bike. For thirty miles, Jan Karski pedalled furiously in the dark. The guide's light would disappear around bends, he could no longer see the road, he fell off, got up again and darted away in pursuit of Fernando.

Then they reached the sea, where he hid in the bottom of a fishing boat; lying under a coat, he remained motionless for three days. He was given food and mulled wine. A second guide took him across the Pyrenees. They walked over the mountains for another three days. One evening, two figures approached them. They thought they were about to be arrested, but they were two Frenchmen, an officer and his eighteen-year-old son, who were going to join General de Gaulle. Jan Karski suggested that they join up together. The next day, they met an old anti-fascist Spaniard, who took them all in for the night before driving them to the station, where the mechanic on the train to Barcelona took them under his protection. So they spent the journey on the deck of the coal wagon. At the final stop before Barcelona, they jumped off the train and split up.

Jan Karski arrived in the outskirts of Barcelona after walking for several hours. He had been given an address and now hoped to find the street by chance. In the end, he asked a worker the way. The man gave him directions then stared at him with a smile: 'De Gaulle?' So Jan Karski answered: 'De Gaulle.' When he found the right address, he gave the password. A little man with rosy cheeks opened the door then gave him some food, before launching into an anti-fascist diatribe.

That afternoon, Jan Karski went to the British consulate. He met with the Consul-General, who knew about his mission and provided him with all the necessary documents to travel to the Allied territories.

From that moment on, Jan Karski was no longer in danger.

He was escorted to a limousine belonging to the diplomatic corps, which took him on the eight-hour drive to Madrid and dropped him off in front of a villa in the neighbourhood where all the embassies were. He received a new set of papers, then took the train to Algeciras with two Spanish bodyguards.

From Algeciras, a fishing boat took him out to sea to a British launch, which headed straight to Gibraltar. He was welcomed by a certain Colonel Burgess and drank a straight scotch with him in the officers' mess. The next day's breakfast seemed sumptuous to him. Later that evening, he departed for England aboard the American bomber *Liberator*.

The flight lasted eight hours. They landed in London, on a military base. Jan Karski was then questioned for two days by the British secret services, who wanted to get hold of his documents. An official written complaint from the Polish government was necessary to get him released. In his book, Jan Karski gives an extremely restrained version of this event: 'It took quite a while,' he writes, 'to route me through the complex English investigation machinery. It was fully two days before I was delivered to the Polish authorities.'

∽

It was now November 28 1942. Jan Karski had succeeded in reaching the Polish government in exile. There now began a long period of reporting. Each day was made up of talks, interviews, meetings and conferences. The sensation of freedom that he had felt on arriving in England disappeared as he started talking about the internal events in Poland: he was then plunged back into what he calls 'the Gestapo-haunted, suffering atmosphere of the Underground'.

It was firstly Stanislas Mikolajczyk, the Minister of the Interior, who received his oral report.

Then he met General Sikorski, the head of the government. They knew each other, because they had met in Angers, during Karski's first mission to France. They spoke for a long time about the future organisation of Poland, and the plans that the leaders of the Underground were devising for when the war was over.

Sikorski decorated Karski with the cross of *Virtuti Militari*, the highest Polish military distinction. Then he personally presented him with a silver cigarette case with his signature engraved on it, and told him to get some rest: 'Don't let all these conferences and reports wear you out. Don't let the Allies do what the Gestapo failed to accomplish.'

He looked at the scars on Karski's wrists: 'They look nasty,' he said. 'From what I can see the Gestapo gave you a decoration too.'

Karski then informed the leaders of the Allies, firstly Anthony Eden, the British Minister of Foreign Affairs. He had been Karski's idol in his youth; when studying political science in the library of the League of Nations in Geneva, Karski had admired his eloquence and elegance.

Anthony Eden listened to him attentively, then said: 'You seem to have been through everything in this war, except one: the Germans did not shoot you.'

Karski met with all of the British political leaders, then presented himself before the United Nations War Crimes Commission. He explained what he had seen in the Warsaw ghetto and at the camp of Izbica Lubelska (which he still called Belzek in his book). 'My testimony,' he said, 'was placed on record and I was told that it will be used as evidence in the United Nations' indictment against Germany.'

He was interviewed by the British press and by that of the other Allied countries; he met with politicians, writers and representatives of various churches.

He soon realised that, in London, Poland did not count for much. The interests at stake were so complex, and the war machine and its economy so weighty, that the Polish situation was a secondary consideration. In fact, who were the Poles? For the British, Poland could be summed up by the short campaign of September 1939, and 'some echoes of obstinate resistance', as Karski put it. When it came down to it, no one understood the heroism of that nation which refused to collaborate with Germany; no one understood that notion of an 'Underground state', while everywhere else compromise prevailed. And then, as Karski puts it, people constantly wondered if the sacrifices of Poland could be compared with the 'immeasurable heroism, sacrifice and suffering of the Russian people'.

In May 1943, General Sikorski informed Karski that he would soon have to leave for the United States, to carry out the same mission as in London: to tell of what he had seen and what had happened to him in Poland. To relay the messages from the Polish Underground and from the Jews in Warsaw. The only advice Sikorski gave him was: 'You will tell them the truth and only the truth.' A few weeks later, the head of the Polish government died in a plane crash in Gibraltar.

⤳

So, before long Jan Karski was 'watching the Statue of Liberty emerging from the waters of New York Harbor', as he puts it. He plunged once more into a series of talks, speeches, interviews and presentations. He met with numerous important people. He spoke with representatives of the State Department. He passed on his information to Catholic and Jewish bodies. He spoke about the fate of the Jews with Felix Frankfurter, a judge on the US Supreme Court, who was also Jewish. Jan Karski does not say so in his book, but a witness to their interview reported that, no sooner had Karski stated what he had seen concerning the extermination of the Jews, than Judge Frankfurter exclaimed: 'I cannot believe it.' 'Do you think I'm lying?' Jan Karski asked. 'I'm not saying you're lying, just that I cannot believe it.' Whether this incapacity to believe that the Jews of Europe were being exterminated in 1943 was a matter of personal incredulity or political obligation, it all came down to the same thing: Jan Karski's message changed nothing, and did not 'shake the conscience of the world', as the two leaders of the Jewish community in Warsaw had hoped.

He was told that the American President, Franklin D. Roosevelt, wanted to hear what he had to say in person. The meeting took place in the White House on July 28 1943, and lasted a little over an hour. Jan Karski was accompanied by the Polish ambassador to Washington, Jan Ciechanowski.

Roosevelt, wrote Karski, was 'amazingly well informed about Poland and wanted still more information'. Jan Karski explained to him the organisation of the Polish Underground in detail. He made it clear why Poland succeeded in not collaborating with the Nazi occupiers. Roosevelt wanted to know if, in his opinion, 'those stories about the methods used by the Nazis against the Jews' were true. Jan Karski confirmed that there was nothing exaggerated about such stories: the Germans intended to exterminate the entire Jewish population of Europe; the process had begun and several million Jews had already died in Poland. Only direct reprisals, such as the massive bombing of German cities, accompanied by leaflets informing the population that their government was exterminating the Jews, could still stop the massacre.

After the interview, Jan Karski walked through the streets of Washington. In a square, he discovered a statue of Kosciuszko, the hero of Polish independence. He sat down on a bench and watched the passers-by.

PART THREE

The Jews were left to be exterminated. No one tried to stop the massacre. No one *wanted* to try to stop it. When I transmitted the message from the Warsaw ghetto to London, and then Washington, no one believed me. No one believed me because no one *wanted* to believe me. I can still see the faces of all the people I talked to; I can remember perfectly how awkward they looked. This was back in 1942. Were they still that embarrassed, three years later, when the death camps had been discovered? They were not too embarrassed to declare themselves victors, nor to claim this victory for the 'free world'. How can a world which left the Jews to be exterminated call itself free? How can they claim to have won anything at all? There were no victors in 1945, there were just accomplices and liars.

When I told the British that the Jews were being exterminated in Poland, when I repeated again and again the same information to the Americans, they replied that it was impossible, that no one could exterminate thousands of people, or even imagine such a thing. Roosevelt himself looked startled in front of me, but his amazement was just a lie. They all knew, but pretended not to know. They all played at being ignorant, because their ignorance was beneficial to them, and it was in their interest to delude others too. But the secret services had done their job, and people knew, and all those who pretended that they did not know were already working for the propaganda of deceit.

I have read everything that has been written on the matter since the end of the war. The British had been informed, the Americans too. They were perfectly aware when they decided not to try to stop the extermination of Europe's Jews. Perhaps, in their eyes, they quite simply should not have stopped it; perhaps the Jews of Europe should not have been saved. In any case, if the extermination was carried out so easily, it was because the Allies acted as if they did not know.

Thus, on leaving my interview with Roosevelt, on July 28 1943, I realised that there was nothing to be done: the Jews of Europe would die, one after the other, exterminated by the Nazis, with the passive complicity of the British and Americans. I sat down on a bench, just by the White House and, in the fragrance of the bay trees, amid the beautiful cedars and acacia shrubs in Lafayette Square, I spent several hours watching the world collapse. I understood that it would never be possible to awaken the 'conscience of the world', as the two men in the Warsaw ghetto had asked; I understood that the very idea of the 'conscience of the world' was now defunct. It was finished, the world was entering into a period when there would soon be no obstacles to destruction, because no one would find it gainful to oppose the destroyers. In this way, destruction would follow its course, concealing itself less and less, and being confronted by fewer and fewer limits, and there would be nothing good anymore to oppose evil, just more evil—everywhere.

Roosevelt had spoken to me about that wonderful future, in which a reconciled humanity would make another war impossible, in which the very idea of war would be abolished. But like everyone else who, at the time, projected themselves so easily into the post-war period, while every day the war was blinding us with horror, Roosevelt wanted above all to avoid dirtying his own hands.

On that bench in Lafayette Square, while the sun was setting, I wanted to vomit. Nausea had saved my life on several occasions, but this time it did not come to my assistance. I stayed on that bench for several hours, wrapped up in a military coat which had been placed over my shoulders on my arrival at New York airport, as though covering up a horse which had just won a race. And while the lights in the White House's windows came on one by one, I understood that salvation would not come, would never come, and the very idea of salvation was dead. And when the Warsaw Uprising broke out a year later, the Poles believed until the last moment that the British, Americans and Soviets would come to save them. But as for me, as of July 28 1943, I knew that they would do nothing. Ever since that late afternoon, I knew that Warsaw would be abandoned, just as Poland had been abandoned in September 1939, and just like the

Jews of Poland, Germany, Holland, France, Belgium, Norway, Greece, Italy, Croatia, Bulgaria, Austria, Hungary, Romania and Czechoslovakia had all been abandoned.

On one side, there was extermination, and on the other abandonment—there was nothing more to be hoped for. This was the world's new program, and sure enough this new world arrived: we have all suffered from this abandonment, and suffer from it to this day. This is why it has become absolutely impossible for me to sleep. Since July 28 1943, that is to say, for over fifty years, I have not been able to sleep. If it is impossible for me to sleep, it is because at night I can hear the voices of those two men in the Warsaw ghetto; every night, I hear their message being recited in my mind. No one wanted to hear their message, which is why, for fifty years, it has not stopped occupying my nights. It is utter torment to live with a message that has never been delivered; it is enough to drive you insane. And so my sleepless nights remain open to the message, they welcome it. I have spent over half my life thinking of Poland, the Warsaw ghetto, the two men who entrusted me with a message that no one wanted to hear. I have spent my nights thinking about those two men, and all the men they represented, about the message that continues to live inside me, while they have died, exterminated; this is how my sleepless nights began. When once in your life you have been the bearer of a message, you remain its bearer for ever.

The moment you close your eyes, at that precise moment when the visible world vanishes, when you are at last open and available, sentences surge up. Night and day mingle, dusk becomes confused with dawn, and the sentences take command.

The words waver a little, like tiny flames. It is almost unbeliev-able, hard to imagine, but they are quite clearly alive, and when they start up, there is a sudden flash, which is trembling and swift, unstoppable as it slips through the eye of a needle. You immediately recognise the voices of the two men in the Warsaw ghetto: like all messengers, you have become the message.

Not for a single day in my life have I managed to think of anything other than the message from the Warsaw ghetto, it is all I have ever done: think about the message from Warsaw, and when I thought I was thinking about something else, it was in fact about the message from Warsaw that I was thinking. In the end, I realised that there was something untransmittable in that message, something that could not be heard, and that perhaps will never be heard. Sometimes I think it was impossible for people to hear what I had to say: no one can bear to hear that a whole section of the world is being massacred, even though everyone else knows about it. Everyone knows that one section of the world is massacring another one, and yet it is impossible to make this apparent.

And then, while I was carrying the message from the Warsaw ghetto to America, the Warsaw ghetto ceased to exist. While I was taking this message to the Allies, those who gave it to me perished. Is it not always too late for such a message? During those sleepless nights, which have opened out in my life, I remain alert: I spend my time refusing the idea that it is too late. Because, with words, time returns. I spoke, but was not listened to; I continue speaking, and so may yet be heard: perhaps you will hear what still remains in my words, and their meaning which comes from even further away than my voice does; perhaps in this message that was transmitted to me fifty years ago, there is something that resists time, and resists even extermination; perhaps, inside this message, there is *another message*.

This is why, every night, I continue to devote myself to my sentences. And if I am telling you about my life, it is above all about these sentences that I am speaking—about the way in which they gave shape to my existence, and gave me a second birth.

I, Jan Karski, born in 1914 in Lodz, Poland, in the worst town of the worst country in the world, in an unloved, ill-treated country, I have not forgotten, I continue obstinately *not to forget*. They continue to heap Poland with infamy, to reduce it to that anti-Semitism which it suits their countries to inflict on it, because it gives them the illusion of cleansing themselves, even though they all collaborated one way or another with the Nazis. But a time comes when respectability fails to mask the abjection on which it is founded. Then, the scapegoat begins to speak and, of course, the shame it is accused of turns out to be shared by everyone. They are all tarred with the same brush. Some even talk about 'humanity'.

At about two or three in the morning, it starts up: names surge up between my lips—in an endless succession. First, the names of the ghettos: those of Lodz, Krakow, Warsaw, Lublin, Kielce, Radom, Czestochowa and Bialystok; railway lines stretch out in my mind, they dig out shafts through which I can hear the sounds from winter 1942, from trains heading towards Auschwitz-Birkenau, Majdanek, Treblinka, Sobibor, Belzec,

Chelmno. I can hear the sounds of the deportations, lamenting men, women and children crammed on top of each other, in wagons in which the smell of shit and piss heralds the odour of death; I can hear them die; death grabs them, and it is like a starving dog leaping at my throat. I get out of bed and go to the living room. My wife remains fast asleep, even with the light on. She knows that, every night at about three o'clock, I have an appointment with my ghosts, as she puts it, and that I have no choice but to answer their call. It is impossible for me to escape from their dead voices: not only would that be unjust, but it would also be like killing them a second time. After all, listening every night to the voices of the dead is a way to make them live again.

Pola understands my insomnia; she is a Polish Jew, her family was exterminated in the Nazi death camps, she was the only one to escape. Sometimes, she is sleepless too, and she joins me on the living room couch, where I go each night, wrapped up in my old coat, and together we look out of the window, towards the Statue of Liberty out there, brandishing her torch.

In the beginning, when I arrived in America, that statue made my heart beat, and I cherished it like all those who have left their countries; as in the Kafka novel, I sometimes confused its torch with a sword, and saw in liberty a symbol of justice. Later, in the post-war years, when I chose to stay in New York while Stalin, with the agreement of the Allies, was transforming Poland into a Soviet prison, I used to stare at the Statue of Liberty with hatred. It was just like Roosevelt, it was like all the Allied commanders, like any other symbol: it lied. I learned to hate the Statue of Liberty a little more every night; I started taking out my anger on it; and it was by looking at its false light through the darkness that I continued to resist. In a way, I have never stopped being part of the Polish Underground.

Recently, during a trip to Jerusalem, a rabbi asked me what it meant to me to be Polish. I answered that 'Poland' meant 'resistance', and that being Polish meant being against all forms of tyranny. A Pole is someone who has fought against Hitler, but also against Stalin. A Pole is someone who has always fought against the Russians, no matter what they called themselves, Stalinists, Bolsheviks or Soviets; a Pole, above all, is someone who was not taken in by the lie of Communism, and someone who has not been taken in either by that other lie: American domination, the criminal indifference which is typical of so-called democracies. A Pole is essentially isolated. This isolation is the only genuine political attitude. So, perhaps this Poland exists only in my mind, perhaps I am the only Pole. In any case, the liberty that drives me has not weakened since 1945, since Churchill, Roosevelt and Stalin divided up the world between them in Yalta, like a trio of vultures. Being Polish, I told the rabbi, is to be a dissident—it means constantly living as if your destiny was inevitable solitude.

Today, so as no longer to hear the voices of those Jews being taken to their deaths, to no longer hear the names of the ghettos and of the death camps which are printed on my mind, to stop that din which shatters my nerves each night, I sometimes recite the words that the two men from the Warsaw ghetto confided in me. I recite them softly, like a prayer; I pronounce each sentence slowly. The message comes back to me effortlessly; I can repeat the whole thing by heart. I close my eyes, and the two men from the ghetto speak for me, their voices become superimposed over mine, they live again. Sometimes, I also hear Roosevelt's voice, a rather grumpy growl, the kind of voice that is trying to sound kindly. Still today, I can hear him stifling a yawn as I spoke about the fate of those Jews who were resisting the Nazis, and the fate of the Jews who were being deported to the death camps to be exterminated.

I had been accompanied by Jan Ciechanowski, the Polish ambassador in Washington, who gave an extremely diplomatic report of our conversation, while, in my book, I concealed my point of view. At the time when the book was published, in 1944, it was impossible for me to tell the truth. The Polish government had read over the text, and had insisted on a few 'strategic limitations'. We were counting on the Allies, and so it was necessary not to annoy the Americans, who in turn did not want to fall out with the Soviets, and so I said nothing in my book against either of them.

Roosevelt had just finished having dinner. He used to eat very early, at around six o'clock. When I went into the Oval Office with the ambassador, they were clearing away the trays. Roosevelt was still chewing, he wiped his mouth while absent-mindedly reading a piece of paper that he was holding in his hand. My name had been written on it in a black marker, as I could see through the transparent sheet; presumably it informed him of what he needed to know about me. Roosevelt walked over, his lips moist, and asked me my name. I found that ridiculous, because he had just read it on his sheet of paper. So I do not know what possessed me, but instead of saying 'Jan Karski', I said 'Nobody'. In the end, it did not really matter, and it sounded almost the same. Roosevelt did not really understand and, while giving me a firm handshake, he replied: 'Welcome Mister Karski.'

There were many people present in the room, soldiers sitting on couches around a low table decked with a white tureen, and, standing by the door, just beside the bodyguards, a beautiful woman in a grey suit and white blouse, with hair in a bun and wearing glasses, was taking notes. We sat down, the ambassador and I, on one of the couches and, while I explained to Roosevelt the conditions for the Poles to be able to resist the Nazis and the Stalinists, he wriggled around on his chair, like a man looking for the right position for a doze. He ended up adopting the same posture I was to see later, in the famous photo of the Yalta summit, in which Churchill, Roosevelt and Stalin are sitting next to each other, each rivalling the others' bulkiness and self-satisfaction—or, rather, trying very hard to look that way. In front of the ambassador and me, Roosevelt looked just as dozy as he was to appear at Yalta. But sleepy people are precisely those who are trying to put you to sleep, too. Thus, he did not speak much during our interview, nor did his aides add very much. From time to time, he turned back towards the woman in the white blouse, and made no bones about staring at her legs.

I spoke freely, I tried to describe what I had seen in the camp of Izbica Lubelska. The young woman took notes, but Roosevelt said nothing. He had unbuttoned his jacket and slumped comfortably back into his armchair. I think he was digesting his meal. I said to myself: *Franklin Delano Roosevelt is a man who is digesting*—he was in the process of digesting the extermination of Europe's Jews. And then, when I repeated in front of him the message from the two men in the Warsaw ghetto, when I relayed their demands about the bombing of German cities, Roosevelt slowly opened his mouth. I thought that his reaction was going to be terrible, but it was not. He said nothing; his mouth remained a little twisted, then he stifled a yawn. The more I went into the expectations of the Jews in the Warsaw ghetto, and thus of all the ghettos in Europe, and of all the Jews who were being exterminated, the more Roosevelt had to stifle his yawns. Each time he opened his mouth, I was expecting to hear him speak. The ambassador and I would at last hear the viewpoint of the USA about saving the Jews of Europe—but nothing came, except a yawn.

In embarrassment, I started staring at the tureen as I continued to speak. I wondered what was in it. Then, after a time, Roosevelt said: 'I understand.' And then repeated these words several times. The way he proceeded was as follows: each time I spoke of some macabre detail that was likely to move him, he glanced round at the woman in the white blouse, took the opportunity to stare at her legs, and then opened his mouth, twisting his lips to the left. As he yawned, the words emerged: 'I understand.' Were the words just there to camouflage the yawns? It seemed to me that, for Roosevelt, words were so close to a yawn that speaking was like yawning. In the end, *Franklin Delano Roosevelt expressed himself by yawning.* I heard him say once more, with his mouth twisted: 'I understand.' What he was stifling with

115

his words was perhaps not a yawn, but rather speech itself. Because, in reality, he *did not want to understand*, it was in his interest *not to understand*. The more he said 'I understand', the more he expressed the contrary desire.

Despite everything, I sensed a curiosity in him, that haughty curiosity that people have for foreigners they despise. After all, the ambassador and I were merely vulgar Poles, in other words, inhabitants of a country that no longer really existed, and which weighed nothing when it came to the balance of forces aimed at ending that global conflict. At the time, I knew nothing about the secret Tehran agreements in which, in late 1943, the British and Americans had given Stalin everything he wanted when it came to eastern and central Europe. The war was not over yet, but Poland had already been sold to Stalin. In Warsaw, my friends were resisting for no reason; Stalin was already planning to obliterate Poland, just as Hitler had decided to do before him. The Poles, in such a situation, were merely an embarrassment, especially as diplomatic relations between Poland and the USSR had been broken off.

In the end, that day, all the ambassador and I were doing was embarrassing Roosevelt, who had received us only to save face. And then we were Catholics, in other words, for Americans, rather like fanatics. So I was almost expecting him to ask how it was possible for Polish Catholics—who were supposed to be anti-Semites—to be working so hard to save the Jews. But he said nothing, and instead glanced once more at the legs of the woman in the white blouse. I stared at the tureen, and started wondering what the ambassador and I were doing there.

I did not know at the time that the best way to make someone fall silent is to let them speak. And that is exactly what happened: I was allowed to speak, that day, like dozens of other times, and I kept speaking for years, I wrote a book, and I was allowed to write it, and when it was published, it turned out to be a success, so that hundreds of thousands American would buy it, and my publisher would phone me up and say: 'We've reached sixty thousand! We've now reached hundred and thirty thousand! We've just passed the two hundred thousand mark!' I thought: sixty thousand yawns, hundred and thirty thousand yawns, two hundred thousand yawns. After an hour like this, I had just one thing on my mind: escape. In front of Roosevelt, in his office in the White House, I asked myself the same question as I had in the Gestapo office, while being tortured by the SS: how can I get out of here?

I had confronted Nazi violence, I had suffered from Soviet violence, and now, completely unexpectedly, I was being introduced to the insidious violence of the Americans. A cosy violence, made up of couches, tureens and yawns. It was a violence that excluded you by its deafness, by an organised deafness that ruled out any confrontations. When I had been imprisoned by the Soviets, I had jumped out of a moving train. When the Nazis had tortured me, I had escaped from the hospital. Each time, in terrible conditions, I had managed to get away. But how do you escape from a couch?

As I left the White House that evening with the ambassador, I thought that from now on it was that couch which was going to govern the world, while totalitarian violence was going to be replaced by another form of violence, which was vague, civilised and so clean that the fine term of democracy could be used to cover it over. And when, in the summer of 1945, atomic bombs destroyed Hiroshima and Nagasaki, I finally understood what had been happening in the Oval Office, where people were so thoroughly understood. Did they have wax in their ears? That was what I asked the ambassador as we left the White House. I thought that Roosevelt and his staff had deliberately blocked their ears, like Odysseus's companions as they passed by the Siren's song. I thought that they did not want to hear, so as to preserve themselves from evil. But I had the intuition that evening that by turning away from evil, by refusing to hear that it exists, people become part of it. Those who refuse to hear about evil become its accomplices, that is what I said to the Polish ambassador as we were leaving the White House.

Just before we parted ways, he told me something that I have often thought over since: 'Deafness is just one of evil's ruses.' Because men act only according to their own interests, and it was definitely in no one's interest to save the Jews of Europe, and so no one did. Even worse: the Anglo-American consensus masked a shared interest *against* the Jews. But I understood that only much later, because shameful truths are always revealed slowly. Neither the British nor the Americans wanted to help the Jews of Europe, because they were afraid of having to accommodate them. Some members of Churchill's staff were scared that Hitler was going to expel the Jews, and then Palestine would have to be opened to them, which was against British interests. In the corridors of the Foreign Office in London, there reigned a technocratic anti-Semitism, in which immigration laws were merely more socially acceptable versions of anti-Jewish legislation.

As for the American Department of State, it was against the very idea of Jewish refugees, and its policy was long based on creating obstacles against any possible exodus; it was only when the policy of Roosevelt's government reached the point of almost setting off a scandal that measures were adopted at last, but the administrative procedures turned out to be so complex that not even a tenth of the refugees that could legally have been admitted actually arrived on American soil. It was only later, when I became professor of international relations at the University of Georgetown, and then at Columbia, that I started to study these questions. And then, in the sixties, my students started writing theses about the relationships between America and the final solution—about what one historian has called 'the abandonment of the Jews by America'.

It is now known that bureaucratic inertia was not entirely to blame, and that there existed a genuine desire *not to act* in favour of Europe's Jews. No matter how incredible it might sound today, members of staff in the Department of State intercepted the news about the extermination and forbade its disclosure. Some zealous administrators even put pressure on Jewish groups so that they would moderate any 'publicity concerning the massacres', as they put it. To their minds, if public opinion was aroused in favour of an action to save the Jews, it would have a bad effect on the war effort, which was the government's priority. So public opinion should not be aroused. And, later on, when it was no longer possible to remain passive, it was Congress itself that blocked any idea of saving the Jews.

When Roosevelt, despite being rather wary about this subject and disinclined to take political risks, tried to relax the procedures that limited immigration throughout the war, Congress opposed him. There had been elections in 1943, and Congress now had a majority of conservatives who were hostile to any idea of refugees arriving, and so would stop at nothing to block America's ports. As for Roosevelt himself, he was not indifferent to the 'Jewish question', as it was termed at the time; on the contrary, he did not want to be seen as being a friend of what was called the 'Jewish lobby', because in the USA at the time this would reduce his chances of re-election. And so the anti-Semitism of the Anglo-American states was based around the impunity of administrative stonewalling.

Whenever a member of Churchill's or Roosevelt's administrations wondered what to do about the Jews, he was asking the same question as Hitler was asking and adopting the same thought processes. Fortunately for the British, and fortunately for the Americans, Hitler did not expel the Jews of Europe, he exterminated them.

When I wanted to go back to Poland after my interview with Roosevelt, I was not allowed to. It was now September 1943. I wanted to regain my place in the Underground, but the Polish government in London was against the idea: according to the Prime Minister, Mikolajczyk, the Gestapo were looking for me and Nazi radio stations were denouncing me as 'a Bolshevik agent in the service of American Jewry'. I think the government was afraid that I would be recaptured by the Nazis. I now knew too much. After all, had I not now understood the extent to which the Polish Underground and Poland itself had been abandoned? Wouldn't it be dangerous for me to spread such despairing information in Warsaw, and for the heads of the Underground to understand their position?

I think the government in exile wanted to continue using my services to spread my message. But, even though I followed its instructions and increased the frequency of my talks, interviews and articles, even though, as stated in my official letter of appointment, I 'took as broad as possible an action with the press and the radio', both in London and America, something desperate had now attached itself to my words. Each day, the same interviews, each day the same incredulity, the same embarrassment on faces, while I used the same words, adopting the same intonations I had used the day before, like an actor. I was worn out. So, between two appointments, I would go to sleep in the cinemas on Broadway; this was the only time when I could relax. The same movie was shown three or four times in succession, and I would open an eye from time to time, soothed by the reassuring repetition of the scenes.

It was at this period that I had the idea of making a movie about my adventures; I suggested the project to the Polish government in London, which at once encouraged me to write a scenario for a 'great film about the Polish Underground', as the Prime Minister Mikolajczyk said in his letter. A pro-Soviet film, *Mission to Moscow*, had just been a big hit, but the Hollywood studios were no more interested in Poland than the American government was. Furthermore, we had no idea how to go about producing a movie; and we did not have the millions of dollars that it would have cost. Having constantly repeated a story which was addressed to nobody, I even stopped believing it from time to time; even my solitude seemed inconsistent. I no longer existed, I was just an increasingly exalted shadow, which day by day tried to convince other shadows that a country was being annihilated, far away, somewhere between Germany and Russia, and that, in this country, men and women were resisting heroically so as to avoid becoming shadows.

It was at this time that my sleepless nights started: a vision opened up inside me across an icy space, and that space was the world. I thought of Szmul Zygielbojm, who had just committed suicide. When I arrived in London, he was the first person, and probably the only person, who really listened to me, because he *wanted* to know—and because, in a sense, he already did know. He later declared on the BBC: 'It will soon be shameful to be alive and belong to the human race, if measures are not taken to make the biggest crime in the history of humanity stop.' This man, whose combative integrity I admired, and who, in London, had moved heaven and earth to save his brothers, had gassed himself in order to share their fate. If such a man had committed suicide, I thought, then the situation really is hopeless. A man like Szmul Zygielbojm only gives up the game when he knows that it is lost; a man like Szmul Zygielbojm fights coolly on to the end, and if he loses hope, despite everything he will find the resources to invent a new form of hope. That is why his suicide, like that of Arthur Koestler much later, completely devastated me. The suicide of our friends deepens our solitude at the same time as it devastates us; the suicide of our friends is all the harder to bear because it addresses our own suicide; it addresses not only our own most secret suicide attempts, but also that possibility of suicide which is always with us. Despite my despair, I continued to plead the cause for a free Poland; I went on endlessly delivering my message, because, despite everything, something in it continued to fuel my passion.

I have mentioned Arthur Koestler. Of all my encounters, this was the most memorable: Koestler had an eccentric, excessive, overweening character, which pushed him into taking part in the most incongruous adventures. He was an impossible personality who always did things his way, and never failed to destroy the slightest link between himself and other people; he always had to ruin everything. Even in my case, even though he was one of the few people who believed me immediately, and relayed my story to the press, he could not stop himself from going too far: he took over my tale and told it one evening on the BBC, thus attracting the ire of the secret services and the Polish government. His early experience of the Communist party, which he had left in 1938 after the Moscow trials, and then of the Spanish Civil War, when a price had been put on his head by the Francoists, gave him the necessary distance to understand what was really at stake during what was called the Second World War. Like George Orwell, he thought that it was above all the metamorphosis of fascism into socialism—the birth of a perversion, whose result was going to be all the more terrible because ideologies would now become confused: all that would remain would be an increasingly obscene devastation, whose political alibis would be interchangeable.

In the end, the twentieth century was to prove him right. And when I started writing my book, it was by thinking of him and of Orwell that I found the necessary courage. This was between March and August 1944. The Polish embassy rented a room for me in Manhattan, and put at my disposal a typist, Krystyna Sokolowska, whose English was as good as her Polish. My intention in writing my book was really to change the course of events; despite the failure of my mission, despite my discouragement, I thought that the world could still hear the messages from the Jews of Europe and from the Polish Underground, that these two messages could still move people, while also influencing the policies of the Allies. I was presumably under some terrible illusion, but at the time nothing would have stopped me from doing what I did. Even Roosevelt's attitude actually heightened my determination. And I also thought that a book could move mountains: if it tells the truth, then a book can change the world; it is the only possible outcome.

Perhaps the politicians had their reasons for ignoring my message, but it was impossible for the world to remain impervious to it. I could still hear the two men from the Ghetto telling me: 'You must tell the world!' But what the newspapers had to say at the time about the extermination of the Jews was derisory. Only a tiny part of the news reached the American people, and even that was generally relegated to the inside pages, or reduced to side columns, as though what was happening were occasional, isolated incidents. What is more, the statistics were grossly underestimated. There was, of course, talk of Nazi atrocities, of their war crimes and of the terror they inflicted on civilian populations, but rarely about any particular organised repression against the Jews. And yet, the news kept coming in, messages were relayed, press agencies provided a steady stream of reports; there were Jewish magazines that published countless articles, and religious organisations that attempted to alert public opinion, but the main press outlets kept things down to a minimum. The systematic program of extermination of the Jews of Europe was reduced, in America, to the image of a pogrom—an *exaggerated pogrom.*

This filtering had become so indecent that, in February 1943, a strange announcement in the *New York Times* caused a scandal. It stated that 70,000 Romanian Jews were about to be taken away for extermination; instead of continuing to obey the Nazis' orders, the Romanian government was offering to help in the transfer of these Jews to any place of refuge chosen by the Allies. Never mind about the motivations of the Romanians, who were almost certainly acting out of opportunism, and seeking out the good will of the Allies because the German Army was showing signs of weakness. The main point was that here was an opportunity to save some Jews. Romania would provide the ships, but demanded a large sum of money to cover the transport costs. The British Foreign Office considered this to be attempted blackmail. As for the American Department of State, it quite simply hushed up the entire affair, announcing after a superficial inquiry that the story was 'unfounded'. It was later proved, during the Nuremberg Trials, that the offer had in fact been quite genuine and had been made by the highest Romanian authorities. Their intermediary, a Dutch businessman based in Istanbul, had offered to organise the evacuation by boat to Palestine.

Would the plan have worked? A lot of money, of course, would have had to be paid. But the main point remains that the Americans did not want to—once again, they preferred *not to want to*. Because by giving their categorical refusal to the Romanians, they at the same time refused to give a chance to 70,000 Jews. They preferred to let them die, rather than to try, by every possible means, to save them. So, one morning, on February 16 1943, a large advertisement was published in the *New York Times* as a reaction against this fresh infamy, beneath a huge headline:

FOR SALE to Humanity
70,000 Jews
Guaranteed Human Beings at $50 a Piece

The text, which was appended to the advertisement and signed by some young people, specified: 'Romania is tired of killing Jews. It has killed one hundred thousand of them in two years. Romania will now give Jews away practically for nothing.' The text emphasised the fact that so far American politicians had done nothing and this was at last a chance to act: 'Seventy thousand Jews are waiting death in Romanian concentration camps...Romania offers to deliver these 70,000 alive to Palestine...The doors of Romania are open! Act now!' The aim behind the irony in the message was 'to demand that something be done NOW, WHILE THERE IS STILL TIME.'

At the time, many people found this message to be irresponsible, and even immoral. But was it more scandalous than the attitude of the American government? Which was more base: this form of irony, or America abandoning the Jews? For behind the abominable nature of this advertisement, which was expressed so crudely, lay precisely the abominable nature of what was happening to the Jews in Europe. It conveyed an idea of the treatment being inflicted on them by the Nazis: they were being transformed into 'pieces', into merchandise that no one wanted. Putting a price on a human being revealed the extent to which, in the eyes of America, the Jews were worth nothing: just fifty dollars, and they were not even willing to pay that much. *The Jews are worth nothing and yet they still cost too much*: with the brutal announcement of this shameful thought, the message revealed what America was in fact thinking; it was an attempt to cast shame on shame itself.

Apparently, at the time, I too used to *overstep the mark*, and certain people complained as a result. When I had lunch in one of Washington's fancy restaurants with the diplomats, politicians or intellectuals whom the Polish embassy had asked me to bring round to our cause, and I started to explain how the Gestapo tortured members of the Underground, when I started talking about the agony of those crazy-eyed children in the Warsaw ghetto, and the way in which the Nazis had filled up that train, obviously I *overstepped the mark*. Of course, I ruined my fellow diners' appetites and their evenings. Because what was happening in Poland did not just concern Poland: in Warsaw, Krakow,

Lublin, or the smallest town being smothered by a double regime of Nazis and Stalinists, those people who were trying to resist were not doing so just to defend their country, but in the name of a freedom that transcended frontiers. And, in my opinion, what was happening to the Jews of Europe did not concern just all the world's Jews, but all of humanity—and cast doubts over the very idea of humanity.

A rumour was going round at the time, according to which my zeal was a mere tactic, part of a propaganda drive intended to obscure Poland's infamous anti-Semitism. So, was I in despair, or full of hope? I do not know—both, no doubt. My despair was as profound as my hope, and did not contradict it. On the contrary, one protected the other. Extreme despair discovers within itself something that unfailingly reinvigorates it; as for my hope, it was boundless.

I wrote the four hundred pages of *Story of a Secret State* standing up, every morning, at dawn. It was impossible for me to sit down: ever since going through the hands of the Gestapo, every time I find myself in front of a desk, I have the impression that an SS officer is going to come into the room and my interrogation will resume. So I woke up very early in the morning and I wrote standing up, my notepad on a chest of drawers. It was a dizzying experience to run through the periods of my life, but I was aware that my 'adventures', as the government put it, were above all the record of a disaster, which was inexorably dragging a country towards ruin.

At about ten o'clock, Krystyna arrived, we had breakfast, then she sat down in front of the typewriter. After that, pacing up and down my room, I dictated my sentences in Polish, which she translated directly into English. I dictated each sentence in Polish, and Krystyna immediately improvised a translation out loud, which we then finetuned together. Having spoken so much to officials, my English had improved considerably, so I then started writing directly in that language, which made our work easier. I was under contract to deliver fifteen pages a week to my publisher. So Krystyna and I worked flat out every day until we were exhausted. After she had gone, I listened to the radio for an hour or two, lying down, smoking cigarettes; then I started revising the pages she had typed, because memories were now flooding back to me from all sides. It sometimes happened that I would get up in the middle of the night to add a detail that I had forgotten, and which gave greater consistency to my narrative. Every morning, Krystyna started by typing a fair copy of my new version, then we started translating the continuation.

There was a bathtub which, strangely enough, was in the middle of the room. I was drawn to this bathtub. It is rare to be able to access good thoughts; in general, our thoughts are piecemeal and shattered. I had my best thoughts in that bathtub: clear, solid thoughts that satisfied me. By filling it with blankets and a pillow, I made a perfect shelter for myself. When I lay down on a bed, it felt as if I were dead. But that bathtub transported me: it was a boat, a ship, a basket. I was carried away towards my tale. Wrapped up in my coat, with my head sticking out, I felt full of joy. Hardly had I laid my body in that bathtub, than I started thinking about my story. I concentrated on it perfectly: I just had to close my eyes to be able to *see my sentences*. It was then that I realised, in the three years that my work in the Underground had lasted, to what an extent I had constantly been crossing a line. I had crossed the borders of Germany, Czechoslovakia, Hungary, Yugoslavia, Italy, Belgium, France and Spain. And then, writing a book was another way to cross a line: a new way to deliver my message, as though I were passing from speech to a strange silence—a silence that spoke. Yes, it was in that bathtub, every evening, that I became acquainted with silent speech; and I can clearly remember the night when, lying in my tub with my eyes closed, the pages about the two men from the Warsaw ghetto came to me. It was in June, and the American troops had just landed in Normandy; on the radio, they announced that the Germans were retreating, and that France was already being liberated. That evening, I thought how Poland would never be on the same path because, after the Nazis, there would be the Stalinists, and they would stay for a very long time. At that moment, the liberation of Poland seemed to me to be as hopeless as saving the Jews of Europe. But, as I have said, despair stimulated me; I would pass from hope to its opposite in no time. The feeling of dizziness was one and the same.

Towards the end of the writing of the book, my publisher invited me to his fine country house, near Boston. It was springtime. A large estate led down to a lake surrounded by pine trees. With joy, I breathed in the odours of wisteria and honeysuckle, as I had in the woods of my childhood. The publisher thought that I looked like a wolf: 'He looks like a wolf,' he would repeat to his friends. According to him, I needed a change of air, I should feed myself up and leave behind once and for all that 'country of the dead', as he put it. In fact, he was right: Poland and, more generally Europe, had become a hellhole—it was the country of the dead. But I belonged to that country; it was hard for me to leave it behind; maybe I did not even want to.

The dinner was sumptuous. The publisher introduced me to all sorts of 'very influential' people, as he put it: important individuals, industrialists and actresses who, according to him, were sympathetic to my cause and might help me. I was asked questions about the war, clandestine organisations, the Nazis, the Gestapo and torture, how it feels to be tortured, and how people manage not to talk. I answered as seriously as possible, but I clearly saw that it would have been better to be amusing. When we came to the dessert, my publisher announced that my book lacked something. I was tired and replied that, sure enough, it lacked a happy ending, it lacked any recognition of the Polish Underground or the liberation of the Jews of Europe by the Americans. There was silence.

The publisher smiled and said that what was missing was even more serious than that: what it lacked, if the American readers were really to appreciate it, was a love interest. The guests burst out laughing. The publisher went on, saying that it was not possible that I had spent four years of my life like that, without once falling in love, or at least having an affair. One chapter had particularly interested him, the one after my escape from the hospital, when I stayed for several months on a country estate in the mountains, in the company of a certain Danuta who was, apparently, ravishing. Couldn't I give my readers a little more? I explained that I had no more to give, because nothing had happened with that young lady, or with any others; there was a war, a terrible war, and none of us had had the time or the desire to devote ourselves to love. The publisher insisted: if we went into more detail about Danuta, if we added a bit of feeling, then the book would be 'more human'. Presumably, to his mind, a book about a man struggling to survive is not 'human' enough.

So it was that I was forced to alter my book, to add a little spice to satisfy my publisher and his powerful friends. When *Story of a Secret State* came out, in November 1944, it was immediately chosen by the Book of the Month Club, which meant that it would reach a large readership. So it was that it was reviewed in all the big American newspapers. Sales in America reached 365,000, it was published in Great Britain, and the translation rights sold in France, Sweden and Norway. It was a huge success. And yet, this book changed nothing. If a book does not change the course of history, is it really a book? My spoken words had failed to transmit my message, and my written words too.

In any case, Poland was lost, because I had hardly finished writing my book when the Warsaw Uprising was crushed by the Nazis. My friends, my brothers, several tens of thousands of insurgents and two hundred thousand Polish civilians were massacred, while waiting for help that never came. They had launched the uprising only once they were sure that they would be helped by the Allies' air forces and by the Red Army, which was on the point of arriving at Warsaw. As everyone knows, the Soviets did not come to the aid of the Poles; as everyone knows, the Soviets waited on the other side of the Vistula, where they could watch the massacre in peace. Nor did the Allies' aircraft arrive, because Stalin was not to be annoyed for a handful of Poles. It was only after the Nazis had dynamited Warsaw, wiped it from the map and liquidated two hundred thousand of its inhabitants, only when all that was left was a heap of ruins, that the Soviets entered the city to take possession of it.

Thus, a few days before my book came out, the Polish government in exile, under Allied pressure, was forced to capitulate to Stalin, *as though they were on the side of the enemy.* As for the Jews of Europe, they continued to be exterminated, without anyone, the British or the Americans, coming to their assistance. Some may say that I am unjust, and that measures were beginning to be taken. But, right until the end, the Allies refused to bomb the gas chambers of Auschwitz, or the rail tracks that led there, under the pretext that their objectives were primarily military, and that such actions would occupy resources that were needed elsewhere. And yet, in 1944, air raids built up in the region of Auschwitz and, on two occasions, American heavy bombers even attacked industrial sites which were just five miles away from the gas chambers of Auschwitz.

I set off on a tour, at the beginning of December 1944, to promote my book. This lasted for six months, during which I was constantly on the road. During my evenings, I spoke to the public in Galveston, Oklahoma City, New Orleans, Charlotte, Rochester, Indianapolis, Toledo, and many other towns too. But what was I doing there? The Polish Underground no longer existed. It was absurd to go on speaking out. It was on the highways of Oregon, North Carolina and Louisiana that I realised that I was no longer a messenger, and had become something else: a witness. I was listened to. No one now cast any doubt about what I said, because a witness is not someone to be believed or disbelieved, he is living proof. I was the living proof of what had happened in Poland. I no longer had desperately to convince anyone at all. People came to listen to me, to see a man who had resisted against the Nazis and had crossed the entirety of Europe with a message for the Allies. I was now presented as a sort of hero. I had become *'The man who tried to stop the Holocaust'*. In a way, I was now a part of History; in other words, I was now in mourning. It is always easier to become famous when it is too late. So it was that they wanted to turn me into a professional hero, one of those people who repeats the same story all their lives, the same story that people want to hear again and again—the story that has made them famous. I presumably embodied the sort of hero that America needed, in order to nourish its bad conscience, because having a slightly bad conscience is always a good way to improve one's good conscience.

So it was that no one stopped me from speaking. On the contrary, I was asked to speak as much as possible, I was made to speak every evening, until my words wore themselves out, until they became devalued, just like all the words in the world. How many times did I say that in Europe the Germans were exterminating the Jews? In 1942, this was a burning issue. In 1943, it was a desperate hope. In 1944, when, in a small town in Texas, in front of a row of respectable ladies, I said that the Germans were exterminating the Jews of Europe, it was just plain ridiculous. I signed books, I met many wonderful people. Some evenings, the debate was lively, because I did not spare America.

I was now no longer held back by any diplomatic constraints. I could criticise America's attitude as I saw fit.

Most of my readership was female, and it was mainly women who came to listen to me and asked me questions. Sometimes, the situation became decidedly comic: I remember one old lady, covered with pearls and rubies, who threw herself on me, saying that she had just read the scene in which I was being tortured by the Gestapo, and that it was the most beautiful scene of all; that moment of torture was just magnificent. After each talk, I was invited to dinner, and everyone wanted to show how sorry they felt for me. In the end, what touched them was not the fact that the Jews of Europe were being exterminated, it was that I felt so miserable. I was the one who touched them, not the fate of the Jews, and even less that of Poland. Of course, they found it all terrible; of course, they wanted the Nazis to stop inflicting such horrors. And then, some of these women were Jews, and had family in Europe. But, oddly enough, when I spoke about the Jews, I was the one people felt sorry for. In the end, what these women listened to, and loved, was my suffering. I sensed that they wanted to do something for me, to comfort me, maybe even heal me. So they never wanted to let me leave, and every evening I had to come up with an excuse, such as a headache or an important phone call I had to make, so that I could be alone again.

What really amused me was the man from the secret services—the OSS, soon to become the CIA—who followed me everywhere, a young man who tried desperately to go unnoticed. Every evening, my talk grew increasingly harsh about the Soviet regime, because the crushing of the Warsaw Uprising had devastated me, and the Yalta agreement was unbearable. It was a second Munich for the Poles. So I now spoke above all about that, about Stalin, Communism, and the misery in store for the countries that had fallen under the yolk of the USSR. And that man was there, sitting in the shadows, noting down scrupulously my anti-Communist speeches, in order to send them to his superiors.

There are some people, even some of my friends, who were convinced that I was in the CIA. I suppose the idea must date back to this period because, when my tour was over, I was asked to conduct a short mission to London. The history of the nations recently annexed by the USSR, in other words Poland and all the others in the 'Eastern Bloc' as they now called it, was likely to be falsified, and the very existence of resistance movements would certainly be obliterated. The idea was to retrieve the archives of their governments in exile and put them in safe keeping, which I did in spring 1945.

Later, when I became professor of political science at Georgetown and then at Columbia, I continued to give talks about the evils of Communism. I gave them all over the world, firstly in Asia, towards the middle of the nineteen fifties, then, at the end of the sixties, in North Africa. This was called 'Information'. So I did do jobs for the Department of State, and I accepted some other missions too. But I always kept in mind the criminal indifference of America when it came to the Jews of Europe. I knew what this country was capable of in terms of abjection, so that my commitment against Communism implied no concession for Washington, nor any real political adherence.

I have always been a 'slimy independent Pole', as a White House bureaucrat once kindly told me. I must also add that I never took part in that infamous police operation, known as the 'witch hunt'. I was anti-Communist because I was Polish. For a Pole, a Communist is someone who stays with his arms crossed on one side of a river, while his friends are being massacred on the other. For a Pole, a Communist is someone who, in the forest of Katyn, presses a gun barrel against the back of your neck.

And then, one morning, I read in the paper that the war was over. I could not believe it: 'VICTORY IN EUROPE DAY' said the headlines. I was sitting on a bench in Central Park, the sky was blue and a soft light was coming through the leaves of the elm trees. But the war was not over, that was a lie; war never stops. It was impossible to talk about 'victory', 'peace' or 'the free world'. What I had been trying to communicate was now spread all over the papers, and the photographs of the camp of Bergen-Belsen shocked everyone. People counted the corpses, it went on for years, just counting the corpses. Of course, the Nazis had been defeated, and Hitler had committed suicide, but barbarity had not been beaten, as everyone was proclaiming. Already, Stalin was recycling the camps that the Red Army and the Americans had liberated. No sooner was Buchenwald empty, than he filled it up with his political opponents, including thousands of Poles. Soldiers from the Polish Army had entered Berlin alongside the Red Army and, once the city had been taken, the Soviets had turned against the Poles and led them into the newly available German camps, or else to Siberia.

I was full of fury, and that fury prevented me from taking

part in the celebrations. There was no victory, there was no peace. No one would find rest, because the difference between war and peace would no longer exist, and murder would now spread across the world. I walked all day through the streets of New York, trying to calm down. It was on that day that I first saw Rembrandt's *Polish Rider*. It is a small red and brown painting in the Frick Collection, showing a young man riding through the dusk on a white horse. I immediately liked the look of him, his proud manner and his nobility; there was something in him that was both gentle and intractable, the true calm of a warrior at rest.

At all the decisive moments in my life, I have gone to look at the *Polish Rider*. Each time, it did me good. Because, most of the time, it is impossible for me to think. Since 1945, all I do is think, and yet I am incapable of thinking. Insomnia has taken over my mind, and does the thinking for me. Thought requires a calm that I have failed to find in my life, except when I go to see the *Polish Rider*. There is a bench covered with blue velvet. I sit down on it. The museum guards nod at me, we have known each other for a long time. They, too, are immigrants, or 'migrants' as people said at the time, generally Hungarian exiles. I let myself be filled by the warm light of the browns and reds, by that grey/green sky that covers the shadows, and which gives the rider a look that oscillates between defiance and reverie. Each time, I observe the entire canvas methodically: the velvety red of his pants, the details of his sabre, of the bow and the quiver, the white movement of the horse, and the glow of that landscape that seems to have consumed ancient battlefields, and made time itself into a blaze, forming the colour of his ruin, and even more mysteriously, of his waiting.

Ever since the first time, what I like most is the horseman's gesture: fist on hip—the gesture of an officer, the nonchalance of the nobleman. I had practised this gesture hundreds of times in front of the mirror, at the military academy, to give myself the look of a young lord; then later with my friends, when I was studying in England to become a diplomat, and later still, when the dream of a free Poland disappeared in the mass graves of Katyn, I used that gesture again, without even thinking about it, and it was like a code, the signal of my return to life. It was my solitude that was speaking through this gesture—and I discovered that it was unvanquished. After five years of war, something of my youth had returned, and with it my faith in things immutable. I said to myself: the unlivable rules, but at the same time something more secretive exists, something intact that withstands attacks and drives you on through to the light.

And so, on that day in May 1945, when the world was congratulating itself, I understood that I was excluded from that world, but something else was being born inside me, or rather was being resuscitated. I was back with my solitude, and once again, because of it, I felt confident. In front of Rembrandt's *Polish Rider*, I thought that it was now impossible to live in Poland, impossible to be Polish, because being Polish would from now on be synonymous with shame, and even if the Poles were not responsible for the extermination of the Jews, they would now be seen as executioners. Even if three million Polish Jews had been exterminated, the Poles would now be mistrusted. And this is how Poland has become a term for annihilation, because it was in Poland that the Jews of Europe had been exterminated. By choosing their territory for the extermination, the Nazis had also exterminated Poland. It is now no longer possible to be Polish, it is no longer possible to live in Poland, because the horror of the extermination has been projected onto it. And even if the Poles were victims of the Nazis, and victims of the Stalinists, even if they resisted against this twofold oppression, the world would always see the Poles as executioners and Poland as the scene of the crime.

That is why, while looking at the *Polish Rider*, I decided to stay in America. I have not had a country for some time, almost half a century, almost fifty years of exile. I have spent my time thinking about Poland, talking about Poland and defending Poland, but today I can say that my real country is Rembrandt's *Polish Rider*. In front of the *Polish Rider*, I look, and listen—I am home at last. If I live anywhere, it is not in New York, it is not in Warsaw or Lodz, it is here, in this room full of tourists, where, facing me, the *Polish Rider* is smiling, where the history of the twentieth century plays itself back in that smile which, little by little, has become mine.

As of May 8 1945, the darkest period of my life began. I took a room in a little hotel in Brooklyn. Insomnia, fever. Without realising it, I started living in silence. I no longer opened my mouth. There was Hiroshima and Nagasaki, in other words the continuation of barbarity in the so-called 'free world'; there were the Nuremberg Trials, in other words the covering-up of the Allies' responsibility. Every time I opened a newspaper, I discovered a lie. Then I needed to walk through New York for two or three hours to calm down. It seemed like it was night all the time; it seemed like I was still hiding, as I used to in Poland. What was I protecting myself from exactly? From insanity, perhaps—from nothingness. I was on the verge of self-destructive mindlessness.

But my head has always been strong, I have never stopped fighting, especially against despair. The embassy helped me out from time to time, but I was incapable of working, or of 'finding myself a position' as they put it. The Poles in New York could not stand me. They said that I did not understand, that peace had now come and I was keeping up the war all on my own. They begged me to turn over a new leaf. But in reality, what they could not stand was seeing how quickly they had turned it over. I was incapable of forgetting, and plunged little by little into that sleepless night from which I am now speaking to you. I had rooms, and walls, lots of walls, ceilings to contemplate, entire days spent staring at a crack. And then silence. I first thought that this silence would shelter me. But when you no longer speak, you are in the front line all the time. You feel every emotion violently, there are no more filters—you are just raw emotion.

But I also discovered that only silence leads to freedom. When you make a vow of silence, you cut your last ties, you escape from everything that holds you back. There is something absolute about silence, a dignity that saved my life. Because I separated myself from others in order to open my heart only to the things that could respond to my distress. For no human being was capable of responding to it, or maybe it was because I was incapable of approaching another human being. Perhaps I wanted to escape once and for all from the deaf ears of human beings, from the obstacles that stop them from hearing.

My publisher was right: I was a wolf. *Creeping like a wolf along the thin wall that separates me from myself.* Where had I read that? Creeping like a wolf along the thin wall that separates me from myself, that is exactly what I did for the ten years after the war. And remaining silent is easier than people think. In the end, no one asks you anything. At the bakery, a few gestures are enough. If you do not want to speak, then people leave you alone. And so, I stopped speaking, I became mute. At night, I could hear a voice telling me to throw myself out of the window, then I watched it as it crept along a crack, and in the end it was the voice that left the room. Silence is a desert, but it is a desert that refreshes you—which renews you. During the time when I no longer spoke, I often had the impression of being in a void. I had leapt into the void, but I had not fallen; I was suspended in my leaping.

As I said: I walked the streets of New York for years, but my solitude merely increased; it even improved. I read widely. I spent my afternoons and evenings in libraries, generally in the New York Public Library, where I had my seat, always the same one. It is not clear to me if I was suffering, because in such regions cold equals comfort, and wandering is measureless. When the sleepless nights started, I experienced what I call the *moment of the spider*. It is not possible to fight against a spider; if a spider aims at your fear, your fear must become the spider. You have first to become that spider, so that a passage will open inside you, and the distance that leaves you unharmed can be adjusted.

Books started to come out about the extermination. I went to the New York Public Library to read them. I read them slowly, conscientiously; as I read, I felt my stomach tie itself up in knots and my throat strangle. It was like with the spider; I had to make myself coincide brutally with the book in question, to be able to rid myself of it. When I went back to my room, after reading a book, I was on the verge of suffocation. So I endured it all, my eyes open, lying in the dark. Then, around the middle of the night, the situation changed: the words I had read entered my blood. I had not kept them at bay, as most people do when they read. On the contrary, they were alive inside me, and I could hear them murmuring. When you stop protecting yourself against the worst, a strange advantage arises: it slips at night along the wall up to that crack that I had learned to love, because it comes from the ground and stretches towards the dormer window, up there, which opens out into the fresh air. And I knew that when I managed to slip into that crack, and also become that zigzag rising up to the sky, I would have obtained what only your adversary can give you.

It is a good thing to persist into the heart of the night, because it is what protects the light: that is what a rabbi in Jerusalem told me, when, at the memorial of Yad Vashem, I was made one of the 'Righteous among the Nations'. I thought that I had always failed, I thought that I had been a living failure since the beginning of the war, but that rabbi told me that my sleepless nights sheltered a glimmer of light, and it was over this light that I was watching. According to the rabbi, *I was living in the darkened glimmer of a victory*. And even if I had not managed to deliver my

143

message, I still carried it inside me, with the steadfastness of a witness who is awaiting his hour. Men die, but words never die, he told me, and my mourning had above all been a way to take care of my testimony and let it echo in the silence. I was silently listening to the words that no one had wanted to hear, and, over time, the words could be heard within me—they had consecrated me. I had been *consecrated* by those words because I had borne them inside me despite everything. This is what the rabbi explained to me in Jerusalem when, a few hours before, at the memorial at Yad Vashem, I had been made one of the 'Righteous among the Nations'.

But, at the time, in the years after the war, I lived on in darkness. Shadows were slowly devouring me and, as I did not want to forget my ghosts, I confronted them. Insomnia protects the memory. For a long time, I was afraid that I would forget my message as I slept. When I crossed the enemy lines, during the war, I was careful not to fall asleep. It was because of the danger, but above all it was because I was afraid that, when I woke up, I would have forgotten. And so, after the war, I continued to stay awake; sleepless nights became my companions. Of course, I have hundreds of memories, there were plenty of fragments, but my most intense experiences, what continues to make me speak, are my sleepless nights. A tunnel, a pallid taste in your eyes, and dawn that sprouts up like weeds. Sleepless nights are like a rainy country.

When it rains, you can hear bells. I noticed that in my childhood in Lodz. If you really concentrate, if you prick up your ears, when every instant is darkest night, when the night is sleepless, and it is raining. Whether you are in Poland or New York, in a Gestapo jail or a hotel room in Brooklyn, whether you are happy or unhappy, abandoned by everyone or surrounded by love, you can hear bells.

Did God die in Auschwitz? One day, I was asked that question, but there is no answer to it. There is never an answer to abandonment, and there is no worse abandonment than that suffered by the Jews of Europe. Not only were the Jews of Europe abandoned by mankind, but they were abandoned by God. The Jews of Europe were the most abandoned people in the world, for they have even been abandoned by abandonment itself. I think my vow of silence was a way to pay homage to that abandonment, and to draw nearer to what is most unlivable: not to leave Europe's exterminated Jews alone, not to abandon the dead. I think only the abandoned can escort the abandoned.

If I remained silent for so many years, it was not only because my words had failed to deliver that message, nor even because they had failed to stop the extermination; it was not just because those words had failed to save anyone: it was to enclose myself in the tomb where God and extermination are face to face, and where extermination silently looks at the absence of God. It was in the silence of this face-to-face between God and extermination, at the very heart of this absence, that I thought I could remain, and mourn. I let all the grief of that face-to-face come to me, I let it invade me, I became nothing more than that grief. I thought that extermination, by exterminating millions of Jews, had exterminated the possibility of a God. I thought that his God knew no salvation, nor charity.

I also thought that he had cursed mankind. That his

powerlessness was as great as the power of extermination. But also that the defeat of his power was not the defeat of his goodness, and that God himself was in mourning, and had condemned himself to silence.

In fact, I no longer knew what I thought. Nothing, no doubt. My head was spinning. And then, which God did I mean? The God of the Catholics? Of the Jews? I shall not speak for much longer about these questions. They are too big for me. The mysteries that assailed me during all those years continue without me, and probably without anybody. Because it is impossible to live at the heart of abandonment, such mourning is inconceivable: it must be impossible to get over extermination, just as it is impossible, at a different level, to get over God, or over his absence. The proportions of such mourning transcend the world, and transcend each person's possibilities.

It was during those years of silence that I discovered the works of Franz Kafka. At once, I felt like his brother. Joseph K. and I had the same initials: J.K., the initials of exile. Here was someone who had heard me. Kafka's ears were not blocked. On the contrary, no one's ears were more open than his. During my life, I have talked to Kafka far more than I have to any so-called living person. It is presumably because he, too, was a messenger. It happens that messengers, in their attempts to find someone able to listen to their message, become lost and stray into unknown lands, and so they discover truths that should have remained hidden; they imagine such fear that it closes for them the doors of understanding, yet opens other doors which are more obscure, and even infinite.

When I met Pola, I had just learned that I had become an American citizen. This was in 1953, I had started studying again and was now going to start teaching. Jan Karski was not my real name, but as I had entered the territory under it, I could no longer change it, and even less admit that it was false: that is a serious crime in America. So, for the rest of my life, I kept my Underground name. I am Jan Karski, former courier of the Polish Underground, and retired university professor. After all those years of wandering, I started to live again. I started going to Broadway every night. I loved music hall. I loved movies with Fred Astaire and Gene Kelly. I also loved modern dance, and it was during a show by a young European troupe that I met Pola. She was dancing with a dozen young people from England, Poland and France, to Schoenberg's *Verklärte Nacht*. From that very first evening, when Pola appeared on the stage of that little theatre in Greenwich Village and, dressed entirely in black, started spinning around, her movements unwinding one by one, I loved her.

It was Pola's solitude that attracted me, the way solitude spoke in her. Only solitude is worthy of love, and when you love someone, your love is addressed to what is most solitary in them. That evening, while a woman was defying the abyss that opened up with each of her gestures, I understood that the only thing able to stand up against such an abyss is love; only something like love can defy the abyss, because love actually exists in a sort of abyss. That evening, going back to my room, after being introduced to Pola Nirenska, after having been troubled by her smile, the smile of someone who has lost everything and who considers that nothing is ever lost, I realised that the instant another person's solitude confronts you, that abyss opens up. It then closes again quickly. But if it subsequently reopens, and opens to the extent that it will never close again, then that abyss changes into what may be called love.

I was so happy that evening that, with my friends and Pola's friends, I talked away merrily, everyone was joyful, those terrible years were behind us, and Pola Nirenska was looking at me, and I was looking at her, and I guessed at once what those terrible years had meant to her, just as she had guessed, at first glance, how terrible those years had been for me, and that only the future could fulfil us, and that this is all we wanted: the future— forever.

She had been dancing since the age of eight. She had started dancing in a school in Krakow, then at the Conservatoire of Music, then in London, after leaving Poland because of the first anti-Jewish measures, and after her parents had left for Palestine. Now she was dancing in New York, where she managed a little troupe. She was pale, blonde and very thin; she had that grace of women made to seem remote by some secret, and she spoke with delicate refinement. For me, she was both the incarnation of the avant-garde, in other words New York, the Village and, at the same time, she was Poland, in other words, eternal gentleness. That evening, when someone recited a Mickiewicz poem, we all wept, but it was not for Poland that we were weeping; on the contrary, if we were weeping, it was because we were all so happy there, far away from Poland.

That evening, I spoke about Rembrandt's *Polish Rider*. Did

she know that, only a few yards away, just by Central Park, in the Frick Collection, there was the most beautiful painting in the world, a painting that spoke of our solitude? Rembrandt had sensed that this solitude is not made of unhappiness, but contains a secret that perhaps can save the solitary from themselves. You have to see the smile of the *Rider*, I said to Pola, because her smile was gleaming in the shadows. That evening, I did not dare tell Pola that she had the same smile, but I did invite her to come and see Rembrandt's *Polish Rider* with me, whenever she wanted.

I waited for her on a bench in Central Park. The foliage of the elm trees was red, and light was streaming down on that autumn day. Pola arrived, and it felt natural for her to be there, as though we had been together for ages. In the Frick Collection, we went straight to the room with the Dutch paintings. The warmth of the *Polish Rider* enveloped us. Pola stared long and hard at the painting, without a word. She was smiling, I was smiling, the rider was smiling. I pointed out the little fleck of red plumage on the rider's hat; she immediately saw in it the blood shed for Poland, and that struggle for independence that runs through our history. And then, in the rider's hat, beneath the braid of black wool, we thought we could make out a crown. So what was that kingdom whose hope the *Polish Rider* seemed to be bearing? It was not that of old Poland; it was a more intimate, almost imperceptible kingdom, a kingdom without land or power, which makes of you a free person.

It was when we left the museum that day, and were walking down a path in Central Park, that I asked Pola to marry me. We hardly knew each other but, for the past hour, I had the impression that we knew each other very well. Because it was not the two of us who had been looking at the *Polish Rider*, Pola said, it was he who was looking at us, and while he was looking at us, he had seen us together, and had seen a couple. In a way, it was he, Rembrandt's *Polish Rider*, who made a couple of us, he had seen us as a couple, and had married us. That is why I asked Pola to be my wife, and she answered with a smile, the same one she had when she danced, the smile that can be seen in Rembrandt's painting, and, thanks to that smile, I knew the answer was yes. Even if she had not said 'yes', it was 'yes'; it was not a 'yes' for right now, but it still was 'yes'.

Later, when we got married, I reminded her of that 'yes' which she had pronounced with a simple smile, the 'yes' of pleasures to come, a 'yes' that I had learned to recognise, and which came to her above all when she was dancing, because then her entire body said 'yes', and this 'yes' extended so far that it seemed to spill out from her body and bend her arms, legs and hair into the twists and turns of an affirmation, and she remembered it quite clearly.

I started teaching at the university of Georgetown. Straightaway, speaking in front of students was a joy for me, and so, along with my speech, I recovered the joy of being heard; the possibility of being heard gave me back my faith in speech. Like ten years before, during those talks when I toured America, I also started listening again, to hear what each student had to say. Teaching brought me out of my isolation and delivered me from my evil destiny; it was when I talked with my students that I started thinking again. I had shifted from obsession to thought.

I stopped chewing over my story like a personal disaster and stopped seeing myself as a victim; I started to view what had happened to me as a more general experience, linked to the twentieth century, in other words to the history of crime.

In fact, I had lived through the end of what was called 'humanity'. You must be careful about that word, I used to tell my students, it may even no longer be possible to use it correctly, because it has served as an alibi for the worst atrocities, it has been used as a cover-up for the most abject causes, both in the West and in the Communist countries. The word 'humanity' has become so compromised during the twentieth century that, each time it is used, it is as if we start to lie. It is not even possible to talk about 'crimes against humanity', as people did in the sixties, when Eichmann was being judged in Jerusalem: speaking about 'crimes against humanity' implies that a part of humanity has been preserved from barbarity, but barbarity affects the entire world, as was shown by the extermination of the Jews of Europe, in which not only the Nazis were involved, but also the Allies.

I was pleased to have recovered my speech, and my lessons in modern history, at Georgetown and then at Columbia, took the form of a ritual for me: in my teaching, there was something of my sleepless nights. I often thought of a sentence by Kafka, one of those mysterious sentences I read during my years of silence: 'Far, far from you, world history is unfolding, the world history of your soul.' This sentence was intended for me, as it was for all of my students, and for you. We think that world history is happening far away from us, it always seems to be occurring without us, but in the end we realise that it is the history of our souls. What speaks to me in my sleepless nights, and which on certain days was expressed in my teaching, is precisely that: *the world history of our souls.*

I did not just teach the history of the Second World War, but also the history of lost humanity. It was at such moments, when I dealt with the heart of things, that is to say not just the strategy, battles, dates and diplomacy, but also the history of infamy itself, that my students raised their heads and crossed their arms. I wondered: have they stopped writing and crossed their arms because they disagree? Is this a protest? Or, on the contrary, is it because they are hearing something out of the ordinary, something that has the ring of truth? Do they drop their pens at this precise moment because they are hearing something that does not interest them, or because, that way, they are sure they will never forget it? I never found out, especially because at such moments in my lectures no one dared interrupt me, and no one came to talk to me when the hour was over.

Every year, for example, when I discussed the Nuremberg Trials, there was a moment when they stopped writing and crossed their arms. I described the progression of the trials, then explained why the Allies needed them in order to whitewash themselves. And, invariably, my students crossed their arms. At the Nuremberg Trials, I would say, no one raised the question of the Allies' passiveness. The Nuremberg Trials, carefully orchestrated by the Americans, were quite simply a cover-up in order *not* to evoke the complicity of the Allies in the extermination of the Jews of Europe. Of course the Nazis were the guilty party, I used to say, it was the Nazis who built the gas chambers and who deported millions of European Jews, who starved, beat, raped, tortured, gassed and burned them. But the Nazis' guilt does not make the rest of Europe innocent, or the United States innocent. The point of the Nuremberg Trials was not just to prove the Nazis' guilt; they had also been held in order to acquit the Allies. The guilt of the Germans successfully implied the innocence of the Allies, as I used to say to my students, who would listen to me with their arms crossed.

You should not believe that the camps were liberated in 1945, I would say, you should not believe that we won the war in 1945: in 1945, we falsified the records, in 1945 we wiped out the traces, in 1945 we dropped the atomic bomb. That same year, at an interval of a few months, there was on the one hand the bombing of Hiroshima and Nagasaki, and on the other the Nuremberg Trials, without anyone seeing the slightest contradiction between them. Thus, 1945 was not the year when the war ended, I said to my students, it was the worst year in the history of the twentieth century, the year in which the facts about the greatest crime ever committed were falsified—the year in which people lied about their responsibilities. For the extermination of the Jews of Europe was not a crime *against* humanity, it was a crime *by* humanity—by what can no longer be called humanity. Pretending that it was a crime *against* humanity means sparing a part of humanity, and naively leaving this part outside the crime. But the entirety of humanity was implicated in the extermination of the Jews of Europe; it was universally implicated because, with this crime, humanity totally lost its characteristic of being humane. We should all recognise that, after the extermination of the Jews of Europe, humanity no longer exists, that this notion is obscene, that we can no longer call upon humanity as a criterion that protects us and exonerates us from our responsibilities: with the extermination of the Jews of Europe, the very idea of humanity died.

At the time, I was haunted by the death of Stalin. I can clearly remember that day in 1953, when his death was announced. I went out and bought a bottle of champagne and drank it on my own, in my room, in tears. I drank to all my companions who had been liquidated by Stalin, to all my friends who had died in his prison camps, to all my comrades executed at Katyn, and, alone and drunk, I softly chanted the song to the glory of Poland that my father had taught me when he, too, had fought against the Red Army in 1920, and the Polish Army had been defeated. Stalin had then sworn to annihilate all of the Poles, just as he later tried to annihilate all of the Ukrainians in the 1930s. But finally he was the one who was dead. I sang: 'Poland is not yet dead, so long as we are alive.' And Stalin was dead, while I was alive.

When dying, during his final agony, Stalin kept pointing at the picture of a lamb on the wall, that same wall in the Kremlin which he had covered with spit the night his wife had died; perhaps, in this gesture of pointing at a lamb, he was identifying himself with all the lambs he had sent to the slaughter. He had always identified himself with his victims, to the point where they excited him, and after each execution he would ask to be told by telephone about how the condemned man had lived his last moments, what his last words had been, how his neck had shuddered. And so, at the moment of dying, Stalin showed for the last time his delight, and how eliminating lambs had been his destiny, how much he had tried, by slaughtering the lambs of the world, to bring down the very idea of being a lamb, so that no one in the world could now say they were innocent, and the very idea of innocence no longer existed. In the end, to his mind, he alone was innocent and, by confusing the victim with the executioner, he was identifying himself in his delirium with a sacrificial lamb.

Pola and I often talked about the Katyn massacre, because we both had friends who had died there. We both thought that the world had not done justice to the Polish officers executed at Katyn, that the world knew nothing of this massacre—and that this veil concealed a form of vengeance.

Between April and May 1940, over twenty thousand captured Polish officers were murdered by the NKVD, Stalin's political police; among them, four thousand were transported in trucks to the forest of Katyn, near Smolensk, about thirty miles from the border with Belarus, where they were shot in the back of the head and then thrown into mass graves. They were not really soldiers, but rather young men, like me, who had been called up in August 1939: intellectuals, doctors, researchers, lawyers, engineers, priests and teachers. By liquidating them, Stalin and Beria were depriving Poland of its intelligentsia and robbing it of any hope for the future.

I had met some of these officers in the camp of Kozielszyna, one of the eight camps the Soviets used for their Polish prisoners, and I, too, would have ended up in a mass grave at Katyn, with a bullet in the back of my head, if I had not fooled them by declaring that I was a former worker, and then passed myself off as a private, before escaping. On the act of execution, dated March 5 1940 and signed by Stalin, Vorochlov and Beria, the Poles are described as 'virulent, irreducible enemies of Soviet power', and they were condemned to death, under the pretext that they were 'counter-revolutionaries'.

The Katyn massacre was class-cleansing: for the Soviets, we had always been aristocrats. Stalin, like all the damned, had a horror of nobility. And here, I do not mean noble blood. My father was a harness-maker. I am talking about the *Polish Rider*. Then, on top of having committed a war crime, the Soviets pretended that they were not responsible for it; for almost fifty years, until the accession to power of Boris Yeltsin in 1991, they attributed responsibility for this massacre to the Nazis, and the world believed this lie—or preferred to believe it. The inquests were falsified, because it was impossible to accuse Stalin during the war, without playing into the hands of Nazi propaganda; then, after the war, the Soviets became masters of the east. When an event took place on their territory, they decided if it had really taken place or not. In 1945, the Western Allies were in no position to enter into conflict with the Soviets, so, when it came to Katyn, the Nuremberg Trials decided to say that they 'lacked proof'.

There was a story, which I told my students every year, because I knew that it would make them stop writing and cross their arms. It was about Captain George Earle. In 1944, Roosevelt commissioned him to investigate Katyn. Earle looked for information, used his contacts in Bulgaria and Romania and discovered that, despite their denials, it had been the Soviets and not the Nazis who had perpetrated the massacre. Roosevelt then rejected this discovery and ordered his report to be destroyed. And when Earle insisted on publishing it, the President wrote him a letter warning him not to, then got rid of this troublemaker by posting him to Samoa. Roosevelt declared solemnly that Katyn was 'nothing other than propaganda, and a German plot', and that he was 'convinced that it was not the Russians who had done it'.

Today, it is no longer state lies that stop me from sleeping, but rather the voices of the dead. If I close my eyes, it is my comrades who died at Katyn that I can hear. It is a lament: is it their prayer or mine? Little by little, the shadows absorb each detail of my memories, which is why I continue to stay awake. I struggle, the darkness must not be allowed to engulf them. Like every night, at about three o'clock in the morning Pola gets up to drink a glass of water, and joins me on the couch where I am smoking a cigarette. The two of us look out of the living-room window at the Statue of Liberty, then she goes back to bed.

When I begin to recite the names of the officers, a ray of light crosses the pine trees of Katyn. It is their names that illuminate the night. Then I *see*: in the gleam of the words, I see their final moments, I see the instant when my comrades will die; they are struggling, some of them try to escape, others strike up a song, and say goodbye to each other. The elderberry trees, plum trees and birches tremble slightly that night. I see the moment when my friends fall into the ditch, when their knees bend and their bodies collapse. I continue to recite their names: so long as their names can still be uttered, clarity will survive. Perhaps only a name murmured against death can take care of its possessor, who once lived.

It is impossible to eliminate a man's life, because a man exists in the lives of others, and what we call time extends each person's existence among all our existences. Right now, I can see in the shadows the outlines of the NKVD police officers; they are in shirtsleeves, they are sweating beside the ditches, the Katyn sun is hot in April. They are weary of killing, performing the same gesture all day, with bodies dropping everywhere and piling up with the others. They have to be made drunk on vodka to be able to go on working. Barbarity is always irksome. The day I heard Sartre's pronouncement, 'All anti-Communists are dogs', I felt like vomiting. I wondered if, for Sartre, and for the clear conscience of the West, the Warsaw insurrectionists were dogs; if my comrades who were executed in the forest of Katyn were also dogs; and if I, too, despite all the efforts I had made to come to the help of the men and women who were being massacred, were a dog.

And of course, people like Sartre know, and have always known, what dignity is; there is no chance of them being dogs, no chance that they will feel ashamed at pronouncing such sentences. That is why the Poles, or those I call the Poles, and who are not necessarily connected to the country, are in such a minority. If I examine my entire life, the same thing has always occurred: *I am part of the minority.* My whole life long, I have never stopped being in a minority. In the end, what I call a Pole is someone who experiences this very same thing: a Pole, whatever country he may be from, is the epitome of the minority.

In the middle of the seventies, when a student discovered my book and came to have his copy signed after my lecture, I was not only surprised, but intimidated: I thought it impossible that such an old book could still be found, or that anyone would still be interested in it. I had not forgotten it, but it was as if it had come back from far away, from a period when no one listened to me, when not listening was part of making war. The students started telling each other my story, and they wanted me to talk about what they called my 'adventures'. Until then, I was just a professor with a Polish accent, the only one who took the bus to go to the university, because he did not have a driving licence. But from that moment, my life changed: it was my students who encouraged me to start speaking out again. They found it incredible that I had hidden away for so long, and that I had said nothing in public since 1945. They understood my silence, but, for them, I was a 'witness', one of the very people I talked about in my lectures: not a survivor, but someone who had seen something that should never have been seen, and who should now make himself heard.

According to my students, I did not have the right to withdraw. I had a responsibility. A witness's life is no longer his, it belongs only to his testimony, and this cannot be stopped. It is impossible for a witness to bear witness just once; when you start bearing witness, you have to continue doing so ceaselessly, your words can never stop, and everyone should be able to benefit from them.

It was with my students in mind that I replied to Claude

Lanzmann. In 1977, he had written to me asking me to take part in a film he was making about the extermination of the European Jews. To describe this extermination, he had decided to use the Hebrew word—*Shoah*—which means 'catastrophe'. He found it more appropriate than 'holocaust', which is still used by the Americans. I thought he was right: 'holocaust' suggests the idea of a sacrifice, as though the Jews were being punished. But the Jews had not been punished, or sacrificed, they had been exterminated. The film allowed the victims, witnesses and executioners to speak.

I did not accept at once, because reviving what I had to say was painful. Thirty years had passed by, and I had no desire to *go back*, I was afraid to dive once more into that hell where speech strips you bare, where you are defenceless, exposed to the shadows. I had spent years consecrating myself to those words, did I have to start all over again? Pola was worried about the effects of such an ordeal on me, and how I would suffer. The return of those words would reopen a wound, which was also her wound, that of her family, that of all the Jews of Europe who had been exterminated. I waited. Claude Lanzmann pressed his point. One night, Pola joined me on the living-room couch, she took a drag from my cigarette and told me how that wound had never healed, and how it never should heal; the worst thing that could happen to that wound would be if it did heal one day, because if it healed, then it would slowly disappear, and one day no one would remember that it had ever existed. If I spoke to Claude Lanzmann, Pola told me that night, if once again I repeated what the Jews from the Warsaw ghetto had told me, if I explained what I had seen when going through the ghetto with them, and how the world had ignored them, how it had ignored the Jews of Europe, and left them to be exterminated, if I told that to Claude Lanzmann, if I had enough strength, then she would be very proud of me.

That night, thanks to Pola, I understood how the nature of the message had changed: speaking out again would be a way to pay homage to the Jews of Europe, and to dedicate my words to Pola's family, and I understood that I, too, in a mysterious way, was now a member of that family. Through my words, I had entered into the destiny of the Jews of Europe, into the destiny woven by such words, into an immense meditation that extends over time. And, since meeting Pola, I had deepened the nature of this connection: I no longer just bore the message, I was part of it. At the time of my vow of silence, I read a large number of books about Jewish thought, but meeting Pola had made such ways of thinking familiar and they were now running in my veins. Here was the very thinking behind our love, and it had made me into a different man; I was still Catholic, but at the same time I was Jewish. I was a Catholic Jew.

The day I met Elie Wiesel, I told him: 'I am a Catholic Jew,' and we immediately started talking about the spiritual life, solitude, and how it is through the reciting of names that existence reveals the abyss we call salvation. No one knows what salvation is, and yet words, or more exactly the word speaks of it constantly.

It was around that time, while I was hesitating before replying to Claude Lanzmann, that the word took on a genuinely spiritual dimension for me. The faith that had been mine up until then had nothing to do with the word, as I had experienced it. I was a Catholic who had had a few adventures in the universe of the word, but there was no connection between this Catholicism and the word, or words I had been using. It was over time that my experience as a 'messenger', as I continued to call it, began to coincide with my spiritual life. And, as I have said, this took the form of a strange religion in which the Catholic in me encountered the Jew in me. I do not wish to go into further details: in such regions, the borders are uncertain; I even think that none exists, the result being that the slightest assertion sounds excessive. Something happened to me, that is all, and I hope that you can glimpse its nature.

During those long years, I had not been protected from my message, nor had I turned away from it. I had continued to bear it inside me. I had forgotten nothing. At no time had those words ceased, and even my vow of silence had been a part of it all. The message had continued along its own way at night, in my mind, and had left me no reprieve. I often thought to myself that, because of the Warsaw message, I was the loneliest man in the world, and, at the same time, thanks to the message I had never been entirely alone.

In July 1978, Claude Lanzmann wrote me a letter in which he assured me of his sympathy for the Polish people: if anyone was guilty of not having saved the Jews, he wrote, then it was not the Poles, but rather the West. He even informed me how, during a recent trip to Poland, he had discovered to what extent the Poles had risked their lives in order to help the Jews. So, I had no further reason to hesitate; what is more, I had in mind Pola's words to me—so I said yes. Claude Lanzmann and his team spent two days in my apartment in late 1978.

Pola was nervous and, when filming started, she was unable to bear it and fled. We heard her car start up and only saw her again that evening. I, too, was in such a state of agitation that, at the beginning, I lost control of myself, and immediately moved out of shot. I did not want to go back in time; it had taken me so many years to extricate myself from it that my body resisted. Physically, I did not want to occupy once more the place which I still in fact occupied, every night, on my couch, just where Claude Lanzmann was going to film me, and which was the witness's place of honour. But Claude Lanzmann and his team were extremely patient and understanding. I told them everything that I had experienced. It took eight hours.

When *Shoah* came out in 1985, I found it admirable. It was a masterpiece. I was overwhelmed, because this movie creates the sensation of the immemorial, and that is exactly the sensation I had had in 1942, when I met the two Jews from the Warsaw ghetto. I still have the same emotion today; it is through this emotion that I am speaking to you. I can see again the ruined house where we met, the two men's terror, their figures among the rubble. We had only one candle between us; they paced around in the darkness—their suffering was limitless. They could not find the right words, because none really suited, and they were on the verge of a nervous breakdown.

When I described the scene in my book, I voluntarily toned it down, because I did not want people to take them for lunatics. They were not lunatics, they were not insane, they quite simply *knew*.

Then, in front of Claude Lanzmann's camera, I relived that scene with such intensity that they were speaking through me, it was their despair that possessed me. By making me their emissary, they transmitted to me their solitude, and this is what I wanted to express in front of Claude Lanzmann. Or, perhaps, I wanted nothing, and it all happened without my wanting anything at all: the words of two Jews from the Warsaw ghetto emerged from me and, thanks to Claude Lanzmann, the entire world at last heard them, the same words as those you can hear while reading these lines.

After seeing the film, was Pola as proud as she had hoped to be? I have no idea. But I was proud of having taken part in such a project. Right from the first few minutes, when you see Simon Srebnik singing as he goes up the Ner, sitting in the prow of a boat, I started to cry. Pola and I wept during the nine hours of the projection; then, as we went outside, she placed a finger on my mouth to make me remain silent, before asking me to promise that we would never discuss it. I promised. I think Pola was devastated, but I also think she was wounded by that film, because, despite its greatness, it was still unjust to the Poles. Claude Lanzmann had kept just forty minutes of my interview of the eight hours he had filmed; I understood that, of course, but the film made no reference to the efforts I had made to save the Jews, which completely altered the meaning of my presence. Claude Lanzmann had kept just the part when I spoke of my visits to the ghetto, and nothing about my efforts to deliver the Jews' message to the Allies, and nothing about the indifference of the USA. Claude Lanzmann had told me that the question of saving the Jews would be one of the themes of his movie, but he must have changed his mind during its making, and concentrated on the extermination itself. This was historically necessary, because *Shoah* now stands as a reply to the Holocaust deniers.

I am probably the only Pole who admires this film because, in general, most Poles reacted violently against it: they reject it because Lanzmann sends them back an image of themselves which they cannot bear—an image of their anti-Semitism. Anyone who has seen *Shoah* will remember the sequence in which a Polish peasant, looking very pleased with himself, tells Claude Lanzmann how, back then when he used to watch the trains full of Jews go past, he used to hail them with the gesture of having your throat cut. Many spectators have associated all Poles with the gesture of this fool. Even though it is true that Polish anti-Semitism has always been terrifyingly violent, it remains unjust to reduce Poland to its most shameful aspect, as though the French were not anti-Semitic, as if the Russians, British and Americans were not anti-Semitic too.

When *Shoah* came out in Paris, the Polish government of General Jaruzelski demanded that it be banned at once, and the nationalist press attacked it for being 'anti-Polish'. As for me, I immediately and unreservedly defended *Shoah*. As soon as I had seen it, in a cinema in Washington, I felt certain that it was a magnificent work which transcended the simple political vision of history. In it, an ancient voice begins speaking, a voice that has travelled through time, defying death. And it is thanks to Claude Lanzmann that I, and dozens of other witnesses, have managed *to make silence come back*—and make myself heard. In a sense, it is thanks to him that I am speaking. And when I went with him to Jerusalem to present the film, during the three days we spent together, it was he who pointed out to me that, on the memorial at Yad Vashem, there are more Poles than any other nationality in the list of the 'Righteous' who saved the Jews.

When the Poles are accused of passivity when confronted with this extermination, it is often forgotten that Poland had been occupied by the Nazis and the Stalinists, that it had not only been oppressed by Hitler and Stalin, but also reduced to nothing by their shared willpower, so that it was impossible for the Poles to act.

It is also forgotten that, despite all this, the Underground and the Polish government in exile did all they could to inform the Allies about the extermination of the Jews. It was not Poland that abandoned the Jews, but the Allies; condemning the passivity of the Poles, in the end, means justifying that of the Allies. These questions still require time: they are part of the future.

In the same way, *Shoah* belongs to the future: we are barely beginning to think about what such a film reveals. Still today, when I close my eyes, at about three in the morning, I can see that old young man, Simon Srebnik, going up the River Ner on a flat-bottomed boat. He is sitting down and singing, like a child. A man is standing up and paddling. It is as if that singing child is being transported towards death. But it also could be taken for being quite the opposite: he is going back through time, his voice is putting a spell on death and, in the distance, in the fields of alfalfa, he will be reborn through memory. The place in question is Chelmno Nad Ner, fifty miles from Lodz, my native town, and

Simon Srebnik is walking along a path between pine trees. He then arrives in a clearing, stops and says: 'Yes, this is the place.' These are the first images of *Shoah*; they are unforgettable.

Since bearing witness in front of Claude Lanzmann's camera, I have not stopped bearing witness. My students were right: when you have something to say, you need to make it heard. In October 1981, a conference was organised in Washington by the US Holocaust Memorial Council, at the initiative of Elie Wiesel, who had read my book many years before and had come across my name again quite by chance. During the conference, I said that I had become Jewish, like my wife's family, who had all perished in the ghettos, the concentration camps and gas chambers, so that all those murdered Jews had become members of my family.

That day, I met Elie Wiesel. I knew his books, I admired his integrity and his casual, cosmopolitan elegance. That evening, he told me, with an air of wicked humility, which he always has when secretly passing down some Hassidic thought: 'It is by the word that life can be given back to the word.' This astonished me, because it gave a name to my resurrection—it made it possible. And, sure enough, if my words had returned to me, then it was perhaps not simply to bear witness, nor so that memory should conquer oblivion: I had taken up the word again in the name of something far greater than memory, which can be called resurrection. I spoke because I thought that my speech would give life back to the dead. Speaking means doing all you can so that the dead live once more; it means rekindling a fire from its embers. I believe that if we never stopped speaking, if speech could fashion itself to fit each moment of our existences, and that each of those moments were reduced to words, then there would be no space left in our lives for death.

I should like to speak for one last time about the shadows. I have something to say which is not simple. Perhaps you will not believe me. I am used to that. And yet, I would like to be clear. Only clarity interests me, it alone makes the word truly profound. Something happened to me that eludes easy comprehension, something that I need to tell because it casts a light over my journey and may also enlighten yours. It is about the Izbica Lubelska camp, the one which in my book I confused with Belzec. At the time when I infiltrated the camp, I could not have known whether it was Belzec or not. The Underground's information was often approximate. We learned things from railwaymen, who informed us as best they could. My guide was one of the Ukrainian guards in the camp. He was under the Gestapo's orders but, at the same time, sold his services to the Polish Underground. He told me it was Belzec, so I believed him. It was in 1942, and none of us knew the exact locations of the camps that the Nazis had concealed in the depths of the forests. This mistake caused problems for me with historians: some have even said that my text contains contradictions which rob it of any credibility. But do historians have any idea of what a camouflaged narrative might be? When I wrote my book, the war was not finished, and I had to conceal certain names: I had to protect the Underground networks.

As for the nationality of the guards, I changed it for political reasons. This was a request from the Polish government in

London, which at the time wanted to spare the Ukrainians; this is why, in the first edition of my book, I talk about Estonian guards.

I am quite aware that going into the camp was complete folly. Even today, what I did seems unthinkable. But I did it out of solidarity with the two Jews from the ghetto, who wanted my testimony to be as good as possible. If I say that I did it out of charity, would you think I was mad? Yet it is true. Inside the camp, the Jews were dying as they squirmed in the mud. The Nazis were shooting them at point-blank range. Men and women were suffocating, waving their arms and screaming. I passed by their bodies; I was there, just beside those who were dying; I felt their breath, I could touch their arms, I was beside them, and at the same time far away, in another world, in this terrible world where we are capable of breathing while another man is decomposing beside us, where we manage to live while a woman is lying at our feet in a pool of blood, where we have the strength to stay upright while children are crawling around us in their own faeces and crying, their faces splattered by their mothers' brains.

I was very far away from the victims; I was among the living, in the homicidal world, and I was hanging on to my life. And yet, I was not an executioner. So who was I? No one escapes from that abjection which divides mankind between those who die and those who kill. All my life, I have tried to avoid that division, to mark my distance from those who accompany murder, to flee from the living who are *just there* when it happens. Because there are victims, there are executioners, but there are also people who are *just there*, and who are present at the killing. They are the ones who then always try to pretend that nothing happened, that they saw nothing, that they know nothing. What is more, if anyone talks to them about murder, they will pretend not to believe it. Whether you were three yards away from the place of execution or thousands of miles, it comes down to the same thing. It is when living people distance themselves from other people who are being put to death that they experience infamy. The distance which separates us from dying men is called infamy, and real life is quite simply a way to face up to this distance.

I have little else left to say to you, and the most important thing is slipping away from me. I have put off the moment of speaking about it, because such a thing would have seemed impossible to you until now. And that is precisely the point: I experienced the impossible. That day, in the camp, I saw men, women and children being stripped of their lives, and I died with them. More exactly, I died later on, after leaving the camp. I had not understood what I had seen in that camp, because what was happening was utterly incomprehensible, in a world where terror takes you, and leaves you frozen. I was careful not to die inside the camp; I thought of the two Jews from the ghetto, and the oath I had sworn to them. That oath saved me: thanks to my mission, it was impossible for me to let myself die with the Jews of Izbica Lubelska, because this would have meant abandoning the Jews of the ghetto and, with them, all of the Jews of Poland and all of the Jews of Europe, whom I thought I could save with my words.

When I emerged from the camp with the guard, we had barely reached the forest when I started to run. I wanted to vomit, and I felt that this nausea would never stop, that it would go on forever. I was going to vomit up the fact of being alive. My body was going to come out completely from inside me, until I died. The meeting place was on the other side of the forest, in a little house where, as arranged, I would give the Ukrainian guard his uniform back. An old Pole was expecting me, a comrade from the Underground. As soon as I opened the door, I started vomiting, as though I would never stop. Inside, I fainted from nausea; it must have been the old Pole who woke me up and laid me out beneath the chestnut tree, behind the house.

Your existence tumbles, it tumbles within you, there is nothing left but a tiny light, in the distance, deep down, almost extinguished, and your sense of sight has already dimmed. Then, a shadow catches you, you are nothing but a moist, dangling rag. Cut: your body no longer exists, and your soul screams silently. The tree comes back, or fleeting lights, then a spinning tunnel sucks you up. The shadows devour everything in their path, then themselves, before dispersing like heavy black clouds. Then your voice jams, your breathing stops.

I know when I died; I can still see that blue and orange mist floating in the foliage, at dusk of course, and my neck felt cold. I was lying under that chestnut tree, beneath a blanket, and everything ceased. My throat choked, my heart stopped beating. The shadows hooted, then flopped down. It was all over.

In the darkness, there was a tiny point, like the tip of a match. This point came nearer. Apparently, I am lucky, I have always been lucky, and this luck is of the sort that disarms death. The tiny point became brighter, it was already floating in the darkness like a newborn flare. The shadows had no power over me. Once again, I was alive.

AFTERWORD

Through my work on the memorialization of the Holocaust, especially at the United States Holocaust Memorial Museum, I have been privileged to meet men and women of distinction. Artists and writers, poets and philosophers, Nobel and Pulitzer prize–winners, titans of industry, Academy Award–winning actors, directors, and producers, presidents and prime ministers, rabbis, priests, and ministers, survivors, rescuers, and resistance fighters—many distinguished men and women of great integrity and high moral character. And yet I have only met one person whom I could truly call *noble*, and that was Jan Karski.

He stood tall, ramrod straight, even in his later years when other men might stoop. He was thin as a rail as if food were of no concern. He spoke with clarity and precision, with a sense of dignity that conveyed his great moral stature. He weighed his words carefully, and now and then he drifted back to that time and place which transformed his life, which shattered his soul. One sensed in his very presence the anguish of what he had seen, the burden that he bore. He had come to incarnate the role of the messenger.

The great Holocaust scholar Raul Hilberg, the dean of our field, published a book titled *Perpetrators, Victims, and Bystanders*, whose title suggested a simple division into three categories of those who experienced the Holocaust. Similarly, the distinguished Israeli scholar Yehuda Bauer suggested that the commandment that emerged from the Holocaust was also threefold:

Thou shalt not be a perpetrator.

Thou shalt not be a victim.

And above all, thou shalt not be a bystander.

Bauer is a man of wisdom. Yet in these searing words, one only knows what one should *not* do. We have come to appreciate specific roles that went well beyond simply *not* being bystander. These roles include such heroes as rescuers and resistance fighters—and these people came to be known as *upstanders*, a word that educators use in contradistinction to *bystander* because it acknowledges their actions. It is a clumsy word, but an apt one, used to refer to the person who speaks out, who demonstrates, who demands that others participate in resistance to genocide.

The honor we give rescuers exalts their role, as it should be—in fact, a judicial process in Israel awards Holocaust rescuers the title "Righteous Among the Nations of the Earth." Yet if one hears their testimony, they often speak of themselves as merely trying to remain decent, caring people in a world where evil is the norm and indifference or paralysis is the protective posture—the shameful attitude of those who remained silent.

We teach our children that resistance took many forms in the Holocaust. Swiss historian Werner Rings identifies four stages of resistance practiced in every country under German occupation: symbolic resistance, polemical resistance, and self-help were undertaken before the final stage of armed resistance. These earlier stages required as much courage and discipline as the latter. They too were essential to affirming honor and valor. Denying the enemy the triumph of their efforts to dehumanize and to destroy the individual's soul and the communal spirit of an oppressed people was an act of great importance. Dehumanization was essential to the destruction process. It is much easier to kill a man who has given up, who has despaired of life, than it is to destroy one who is valiantly defending his existence.

Jan Karski was just such a defender of life. He was *The Messenger*. The title of the book is chosen wisely. A member of the Polish underground, he brought news to the Polish government-in-exile of what was happening in the homeland. He was a genuine Polish hero, a gallant man who struggled for his beloved land and also for the Jews whose voice he became at their most critical moment. That might have been sufficient for a lesser man, but not for Karski. As you will read in this book, he was asked to carry a message of the fate of the Jews, and boldly decided that his word would only be credible if he saw what happened firsthand.

Jan Karski was not his name at birth. It was his name *de guerre*. Jan Kozielewski was a diplomat by training, recruited into the Polish underground by his brother, a ranking Polish Security official in Warsaw. Blessed with an exceptional memory, he was trusted by political forces in Poland and could compartmentalize his intelligence information, sharing only the knowledge intended for a particular recipient. He knew much and said little, but what he said was essential. Arrested, he withstood torture. He slit his wrists to ensure his own silence. Rescued, he continued his underground activities.

On the eve of what turned out to be his last mission abroad, Karski was asked to carry information regarding the Jews in Warsaw to London. Two Jewish leaders who ordinarily would be at odds with each other pled with him to deliver their message: One was a Bundist, who had envisioned a future in which Jews were a respected minority in an independent democratic Poland, and the other a Zionist, who saw the an independent nation in Palestine as the only viable future for the Jews. Yet under the circumstances, their differences were immaterial. The men were desperate. They wanted Karski to carry their entreaty to the world. They asked him to call upon the Allied governments to stop the murder of the Jews, not requesting but *demanding*:

- A public announcement stating that preventing the physical extermination of the Jews was part of the allied war strategy;

- All available data on the Jewish ghettos, concentration camps,
  names of German officials directly involved in the crimes, statistics, facts, and methods in use, such as gassing and death camps
  be specified;

- Public appeals be made to the German people to apply pressure
  on their government to stop the extermination;

- If the genocide continued and the German masses did not rise up to
  stop it, they would be considered collectively responsible for it;

- In the event that none of the other steps forced a halt in the genocide program, the Allies were to carry out reprisals in two forms:
  through the bombing of selected sites of German cultural importance and through the execution of Germans in Allied hands who
  still professed loyalty to Hitler after learning of his crimes.

Karski said: "Your demands are against international law. I know
the British. They will not do this. Making these demands will weak-
en your case. It is hopeless."

The Zionist responded: "Say it. We don't know what is realistic
or not realistic. We are dying here."

Karski at last agreed. But first, to add to his credibility, he entered the ghetto, twice. Once the home of more than 400,000 Jews,
the Warsaw ghetto had been nearly emptied of its inhabitants. Almost 300,000 Jews were deported to Treblinka in seven weeks, beginning July 23, 1942. The ghetto, Karski saw, was a place of squalor, disease, and despair. He recalled: "It was not a world. There
was no humanity. Streets full, full. Apparently all of them lived in
the street . . . Selling, begging each other. Crying and hungry."

He was also transported to a juncture where the death trains were
headed for Belzec. Entering in the uniform of a Ukrainian guard, he
was unprepared to witness what he saw and fled immediately, fearing
that his visceral reaction to the horror would betray him as an outsider.

Then he became a messenger on a diplomatic mission for his

country, seeking to garner support for the Polish government-in-exile and for an independent Poland after the war. Ultimately this was a mission on behalf of the dying Jewish people.

When he arrived in the West, Karski transmitted his messages on behalf of the Poles; he spoke to Jewish and Allied leaders in London, including Anthony Eden, the British Foreign Secretary. He was then sent to the United States to meet with American leaders. To orchestrate a meeting with President Franklin Delano Roosevelt, Karski met in the Polish Embassy with three American Jewish governmental officials, men close to the president: Benjamin Cohen, Roosevelt's advisor, Oscar Cox, assistant solicitor general and, most importantly, Supreme Court Justice Felix Frankfurter, who had helped shape the New Deal. All three were attentive during the meeting hosted by the Polish ambassador at his residence. Afterward, two of the men left, shaken. Justice Frankfurter lingered.

The justice said: "A man like me speaking to man like you must be totally frank. So I must say, I am unable to believe you."

Polish Ambassador Ciechanowski erupted: "Felix, you don't mean it. How can you call him a liar to his face? The authority of my government is behind him. You know who he is."

"Mr. Ambassador, I did not say the man is lying. I said I am unable to believe him. There is a difference."

How are we to understand Frankfurter's inability to believe the messenger from Poland? Zbigniew Brezinski, who later became President Jimmy Carter's national security advisor, was but a twelve-year-old boy when Karski visited his father, who was then a Polish diplomat in Canada. He recalled:

As a young boy, I sat at a supper in my house in Canada listening to Jan Karski telling my family about the total extinction of the Jews in Poland. I recall to this day the stunning incomprehension that his report generated for it seemed so beyond any historical experience to which we could relate. In other words, we did not believe him, but it was almost impossible to comprehend what was actually transpiring.

Brezinski compared it to only one other moment in his life. Within days of becoming national security advisor, he asked for a briefing on the doomsday scenario of nuclear war. He recalled that then too—as with Karski—he could not comprehend what was being said. The first time he was a child, the second time he was a man of immense responsibility, and yet the feeling was the same.

Karski finally met with President Franklin Delano Roosevelt. Roosevelt found little interest in an independent post-war Poland and even less interest in saving the Jews. Both were peripheral to the global battle against Hitler. Karski left the White House knowing his urgent plea would go unheeded.

Public exposure in the United States made it impossible for Karski to return to Europe, so he spent the rest of the wartime period writing and lecturing. His memoir, *Story of a Secret State*, made the bestseller list and was chosen by the Book of the Month Club. He appeared in *The New York Times*, *American Mercury*, and *Harper's Bazaar*. He spoke in front of more than two hundred audiences from Rhode Island to Florida. "In all of them, I spoke about the Jewish tragedy," he said. "Each lecture was reviewed by the local press . . . The Lord assigned me a role to speak and to write during the war—as it seemed to me it might help. It did not." He continued:

> Furthermore, when the war came to its end, I learned that the governments, the leaders, the scholars, the writers did not know what had been happening to the Jews. They were taken by surprise. The murder of six million innocents was a secret.
>
> Then I became a Jew. Like the family of my wife . . . all murdered Jews became my family.
>
> But I am a Christian Jew. I am a practicing Catholic. Although

I am not a heretic, still my faith tells me that the second original sin has been committed by humanity: through commission or omission or self-imposed ignorance or insensitivity, or hypocrisy, or heartless rationalization.

This sin will haunt humanity to the end of time.

It does haunt me and I want it to be so.

Karski and I had a special bond. I was there when he first spoke after years of silence at a prominent Washington synagogue. I was there again three years later at the International Conference of Liberators convened by the then nascent United States Holocaust Memorial Council. He spoke at the State Department auditorium, where the audience was hushed; his work during the war was still unknown to many, but his testimony sucked all the air out of the room; we were transported back to that place and to that time.

While working at the United States Holocaust Memorial Museum, I taught at Georgetown for fifteen years. Each year, when I taught a course about the Holocaust, I had my students see the movie Shoah, where they heard Karski's testimony. Inevitably, one of them would bump into Karski on the university campus, and one year, a student walked up to him and blurted out: "I know you. I saw you in a film. I thought you were dead."

Karski called the very next day: "Professor Berrrenbaum," he said in his heavy Polish accent, rolling his Rs. "Tell your students that I am very much alive. There will be plenty of time for me to be dead." And we laughed.

Jacek Nowakowski and I were at the museum with Jan Karski when we had ceremonies honoring two Polish Jews. In honor of Michael Klepfisz, we added to the museum's collection a *Virtuti Militari*, a medal signifying the highest military distinction given by the Polish government. Klepfisz was the only ghetto fighter to receive the award posthumously from the Polish government in exile. We also were together when the museum honored Shmuel Zygelboim, the Bund representative to the Polish National Council in London. We paid tribute by displaying his suicide letter; Zygelboim took his own life after learning about the defeat of the Warsaw Ghetto Uprising, shortly after meeting with Karski and learning directly of the fate of Polish Jews—his own family among them—and ascertaining that little would be done to save the Jews. Zygelboim wrote:

> Let my death be an energetic cry of protest against the indifference of the world, which witnessed the extermination of the Jewish people without taking any steps to prevent it. I hope that my death may jolt the indifference of those who, perhaps even in this extreme moment, could save the Jews who are still alive in Poland.

Karski felt guilty to the end of his days that the words he conveyed to Zygelboim caused his death. He also felt guilty after reading E. Thomas Wood's important biography of Karski, *How One Man Tried to Stop the Holocaust*, in which Karski first learned that some resistance fighters who rescued him were caught and executed.

It is a paradox of the Holocaust that the innocent feel guilty, and the guilty, innocent.

Claude Lanzmann's Shoah brought Karski additional prominence. In his own way, the great French existentialist documentarian forced Karski to confront what he had seen—to see it again, to approach what had been repressed. The film did not highlight Karski's by-then oft-repeated recollection of his meeting with the president, or with Anthonly Eden, the British foreign minister. Instead Lanzmann "forced" Karski back into the Warsaw Ghetto to describe a world of Jews anticipating their own imminent death. His struggled for words, flailed and suffered, then ran from the room. But Lanzmann was persistent, unrelenting. He sent Karski back to the camera and insisted that he speak.

If Karski and I were close we brought out the best in each other—my friend Jacek Nowakowski shared an even more special bond of friendship with him. They were both Polish Americans.

They could speak in their native tongue, and they understood each other intuitively.

Jacek recalled two extraordinary moments with Karski that he shared with me. Karski had dinner at Jacek's home the evening that he was diagnosed with the illness that was to end his life. They spent the evening together, yet Jacek was unaware that Karski had decided to welcome his death rather than to struggle to defeat it one more time. He had refused all treatment. He was agitated with the world but at peace with his God, ready to return to his wife, who had died several years before.

Jacek was also present when Karski left this world. It is comforting to know that he did not die alone. His friend was there; so too was a member of the Polish embassy, the representative of a free, independent, democratic Poland, the dream of Karski's youth, the realization he lived to see.

Karski's stature as a self-described Christian Jew is one I have always respected, even as I know it is theologically impossible. Yet Karski defied categories, he resisted classification. When he finally died, the Jewish community in Poland sent a Jewish star from Warsaw, which was placed in his coffin. He would have appreciated the gesture and received star with pride. They made him an honorary Jew—he was one of them.

At the end of his funeral, I recited the Kaddish, the Jewish prayer for the dead, which never speaks of death but of magnifying and sanctifying the name of God, which Karski did with his every being.

The Messenger introduces another generation to Jan Karski—as task that is urgent—and for this we are deeply grateful. To be in the presence of nobility, even at a distance, is to be ennobled.

Michael Berenbaum
Los Angeles, California